# LEAGUE of ARCHERS

EVA HOWARD

**ALADDIN**
New York London Toronto Sydney New Delhi

ALADDIN

An imprint of Simon & Schuster Children's Publishing Division

1230 Avenue of the Americas, New York, New York 10020

First Aladdin hardcover edition December 2016

Text copyright © 2016 by Working Partners Limited

Jacket illustration copyright © 2016 by Charlie Bowater

For information about special discounts for bulk purchases, please contact Simon & Schuster Special Sales at 1-866-506-1949 or business@simonandschuster.com.

The Simon & Schuster Speakers Bureau can bring authors to your live event. For more information or to book an event contact the Simon & Schuster Speakers Bureau at 1-866-248-3049 or visit our website at www.simonspeakers.com.

Jacket designed by Jessica Handelman

Interior designed by Mike Rosamilia

The text of this book was set in Adobe Garamond Pro.

Manufactured in the United States of America 1116 FFG

2  4  6  8  10  9  7  5  3  1

Library of Congress Cataloging-in-Publication Data

Names: Howard, Eva, author.

Title: League of archers / by Eva Howard.

Description: First Aladdin hardcover edition. | New York : Aladdin, 2016. |

Series: League of archers ; 1 | Summary: "Ellie Dray has grown up idolizing Robin Hood but when the famous outlaw is killed right before her eyes—and she is accused of his murder—she finds herself questioning all she thought she knew. Now an outlaw herself, she and her friends must fight to clear her name and stop the local baron's evil plans"—Provided by publisher.

Identifiers: LCCN 2015049319 (print) | LCCN 2016022342 (eBook) | ISBN 9781481460378 (hc) | ISBN 9781481460392 (eBook)

Subjects: | CYAC: Archery—Fiction. | Outlaws—Fiction. | Adventure and adventurers—Fiction. | Robin Hood (Legendary character)—Fiction. |

BISAC: JUVENILE FICTION / Fairy Tales & Folklore / Adaptations. | JUVENILE FICTION / Action & Adventure / General. | JUVENILE FICTION / Historical / Medieval.

Classification: LCC PZ7.1.H6875 Le 2016 (print) | LCC PZ7.1.H6875 (eBook) |

DDC [Fic]—dc23

LC record available at https://lccn.loc.gov/2015049319

*Special thanks to Melissa Albert.*
*For my parents.*

# 1

ELLIE PRESSED HER BACK AGAINST THE ABBEY wall, feeling the cool of the stone through her habit. The air was stifling, thick with boiling water and hot herbs, as it always was in the hospital wing. Today the scent of garlic and butter mixed unpleasantly with the stench of unwashed bodies and disease. It made Ellie so nauseated she thought she would never eat garlic again.

There were eight beds in the hospital, each filled with a figure huddled beneath the blankets. Ellie was beside the table where they kept the medicines—sprigs of nettle and thyme, honey and candle wax, a stack of fresh linen cloths, and a knife resting in a bowl of water, ready for bloodletting. Sister Joan was carefully spooning powders and pastes from various pots and jars into a white ceramic bowl.

"Now you add just a pinch of arsenic to the poultice, girls, but just a *pinch*. Do you see?"

"Yes, Sister Joan," said Novice Agnes sweetly. She was hovering attentively beside the older nun. "You're a very good teacher."

*I won't roll my eyes*, Ellie thought. *It's not befitting of a novice nun.*

It wasn't that she didn't like Novice Agnes. Or that she didn't want to help the people in the hospital. It was just that Agnes was so *perfect*. Her long yellow hair was always hidden neatly beneath her wimple, while strands of Ellie's had straggled out of hers and now lay sweaty on her cheeks.

*As out of place as a duck in a flight of swans.* The image made her smile. She pictured the breeze off the duck pond that lay a mile from the abbey, on the edge of Sherwood Forest, lifting from the water and ruffling her hair. She'd been a novice at Kirklees for four years, but she never went a quarter of a day without longing for the freedom of Sherwood.

Her smile widened. The shadows were lengthening against the bare hospital walls, and it wasn't long now until the forest would be hers—at least for a few hours.

Sister Joan was looking at her. Ellie snapped to attention.

"Elinor, I hope that grin on your face means you know the answer to my question." The tall nun frowned down at her, lines crinkling her doughy face.

"Oh!" Ellie bit her lip. What had Sister Joan been talking about? "I . . . I . . ."

Her search for an answer was interrupted by a painful barking sound. In the nearest bed a little boy sat up, coughing into his hands. With a final, racking burst, he choked up a mouthful of blood.

Agnes gasped, her face pale.

"The good Lord save him," whispered Sister Joan, clutching the edge of the table.

But Ellie was already moving, seizing one of the cloths and rushing toward the boy's bed.

He had fallen back onto his pillows, shivering weakly. His eyes locked on hers, dark and fearful. "It's all right," Ellie said soothingly, dabbing the blood from his mouth.

Sister Joan hurried over, her composure recovered, bringing a pitcher of steaming water. Ellie dipped the cloth in it, washing the blood from the child's face and hands.

"Bring him something to drink," said Sister Joan. With shaking hands Agnes offered a cup of weakened wine, which Sister Joan tipped into the boy's mouth.

"There's little more we can do for him, poor soul," she murmured.

A familiar, desperate sadness settled in Ellie's chest. There was little they could ever do. No matter their patients' symptoms, Ellie knew what was really wrong with them, what made them so weak and susceptible to sickness in the first place: hunger. Thanks to Lord de Lays, the baron who ruled the land on which the abbey and the nearby village sat, people lived and died in poverty, most of them never knowing what it felt like to have a full stomach.

But thanks to Ellie, at the abbey they were fed plentifully. Tomorrow she would make sure the boy had as much to eat as he wanted.

"What's your name?" she asked gently.

"Gregory."

"Gregory what?"

"Gregory Carpenter. My mum's Mary and my dad's John. But he's dead."

When Ellie heard the names, she could picture their house, from her life before she came to Kirklees. Not even a cottage, it was more of a hovel, one dark room full of hungry children and their desperate mother.

"My dad's dead too," she told him. The boy's eyes flickered with interest, but Ellie shied away from the memory—her tale would do nothing to raise the boy's spirits. "How would you like to hear a story?" she said instead. "A proper adventure?"

He nodded and settled back, his hands unfisting from the sheets. Ellie thought for a moment, settling on the edge of the boy's bed, and began. "Many, many years ago the Sheriff of Nottingham decided to hold a contest."

"You forgot to say 'once upon a time,'" the boy whispered, his eyes bright. "That's how all stories start."

"Not the real ones. This story really happened." Ellie began again: "The Sheriff of Nottingham thought he was the most powerful man in the land, after the king, but he was wrong. Do you know why?"

The little boy shook his head.

"Because no matter what he did, or how many armies he commanded, he could always be outsmarted by one man. Robin Hood." Just saying the name gave her a warm feeling in her stomach, like she'd eaten a bowl of hot stew. "The sheriff had declared Robin an outlaw, for the crime of stealing from the rich to help the poor. He put a price on Robin's head so big, every coward in the county wanted a piece of it. You could see the sheriff's notices nailed to every other tree: 'Wanted: Robin Hood, dead or alive'!"

Behind her, Sister Joan tutted her tongue. Ellie

lowered her voice. "Anyway, he didn't have a bit of luck catching Robin, because Robin was too fast and too smart, and he had Maid Marian and the Merry Men to help him."

"The Merry Men?"

"That's right. They were brave outlaws just like Robin, and they made their camp in the heart of the forest, at the Greenwood Tree. So one day the sheriff wakes up and says to himself"—Ellie screwed up her brow and made her voice go low—"'I know how to catch Robin. I'll hold an archery contest, and I'll make the reward one no outlaw could resist: a silver arrow.' Because it was known that Robin could shoot a sparrow through the heart at a hundred paces, and would never resist the chance to win silver he could use to help the hungry.

"And the sheriff was right. But Robin, of course, was far cleverer than him. He entered the contest, but he did it in disguise. He dressed as an old, old man, with ashes in his beard and a hunch. On the day of the contest he leaned on a stick and watched the other men shoot. Then, when it was his turn, he walked forward under the eyes of the sheriff and all his fiercest men."

There was movement from the doorway. Ellie glanced up to see the mother abbess, head of their order at Kirklees, enter the room. She moved from bed to bed, settling blankets or saying a soft word to each patient. She looked at them with the same love she'd shown when she gathered Ellie from the village, just after she'd been made an orphan. Her kindness was the steady light that led Ellie out of her grief, and kept her hoping that one day life at the convent would feel natural to her.

"Then what?" the boy muttered sleepily. "What happened next?"

Ellie moved her attention back to his drowsy face. "He shot bravely and hit the center of the target—but that was just the contest's first round. For every round the target was moved back, until only three men remained: Robin in his disguise, and two hooded men who didn't give their names. The Sheriff of Nottingham gave an evil grin because he was certain one of the three men was Robin Hood."

Across the room the abbess lifted her head sharply. Ellie wondered why, then realized the boy's ragged breath had gone even. He was asleep.

"Well," said Sister Joan quietly. "Your storytelling is a bit bloody for my taste, but our patient seemed to like it." She bestowed on Ellie a smile of approval usually reserved for Agnes. "Now hurry, or you'll be late for compline prayer."

"I'm just coming," Ellie said.

As soon as Sister Joan and Novice Agnes were out of

sight, Ellie ran to the laundry room at the mouth of the hospital wing. From beneath a stack of coarse linens, boiled clean and scented with lavender, she pulled out her yew-wood bow and a quiver full of arrows. She let herself enjoy the familiar weight of them in her hands for a moment. Then she tucked them under her habit and sped toward the kitchen. She couldn't wait to be out hunting tonight.

# 2

THE PRAYER BELL TOLLED AS ELLIE STASHED
her bow and arrow in the tangled ivy just outside the
kitchen door. She lifted the skirt of her habit in her hands
and sprinted toward the chapel, eager to get through the
day's last duty.

Well, the day's last duty as a novice nun.

She came to an abrupt stop just outside the chapel,
breathing hard, then slipped into the back pew beside
Sister Joan and Novice Agnes. Sister Joan sighed audibly,
and Agnes looked straight ahead, a placid smile on her
face.

With her bloodhound's nose for Ellie's misdeeds,
Sister Mary Ursula turned to glare at her from the front

pew. Ellie smiled back as sweetly as she could muster. Even if Ellie had been first to every service, Sister Mary Ursula would still have found fault.

The mother abbess stood at the altar, her face soft over her Bible and her eyes downcast. The jeweled Bible and the chapel's fine windows were the last of Kirklees Abbey's treasures. Even the candlesticks had been sold along with the hangings and the art.

"Into your hands, Lord, I commend my spirit." Each time the abbess spoke, it was as if she were reading the words anew.

"Into your hands, Lord, I commend my spirit," the kneeling women chorused back. The words were as familiar to Ellie as her own rough hands. Life at Kirklees was hard, but the people in it were dear to her—almost as dear as the memories of her parents, which she pushed away each night as she fell asleep.

There was Sister Bethan, singing while she cooked—hymns when Sister Mary Ursula was close enough to hear, folk songs about valor and heartbreak when she wasn't. Less beloved was Sister Mary Ursula herself, the daughter of a nobleman who, Ellie heard, had lost his fortune and then his life in gambling dens. But to hear Sister Mary Ursula speak—and scold—you'd think she was the daughter of the king. Sister Ethel, small as a sparrow and deaf as a post, had the magical ability to sense mischief but a heart too soft to punish you for it. And Ellie's closest friend at the abbey had been a novice named Beatrice, who had lived with them for almost two years. Like Ellie, she was an orphan, but she had an easy laugh and a way with their tiny herd of goats. She was fifteen when she arrived, and seventeen when she ran away to Nottingham with a blacksmith's apprentice. Sister Mary Ursula's eyes still burned with a righteous fire whenever Beatrice's name came up. Ellie wondered if it was the green flames of envy.

A bead of sweat ran from her hairline to her lip. She swiped a hand quickly across her face, then glanced down the row of nuns beside her. Each clasped her hands in placid prayer, ignoring the midsummer heat seeping through the leaded-glass windows.

She was the only one, she knew, planning to sneak out that night. Ellie meant no disrespect to God—or to the mother abbess—but her day was far from over. While the other nuns retired to their narrow chambers and their final, solitary prayers, she'd exchange her robes and headdress for dark leggings and a rough tunic. She'd slip through the abbey's cool halls, avoiding the eagle eye and sharp tongue of Sister Mary Ursula, all too happy to tattle on her for being out of bed late—or, heaven forfend, for wearing boys' hunting clothes unsuitable for *any* lady, especially a novice nun. She'd pass through the kitchen and out the back door, where she'd retrieve her bow and arrows from the ivy. Then it was just a quick sprint past the vegetable plots and under a clutch of fruit trees to the abbey wall, where a well-placed crab apple branch gave her the perfect stepping stool over the worn brick.

And then: freedom.

Ellie started as the far-off ringing of a bell cut through her thoughts. Stranger still, the frantic scraping of metal on wood—someone beating at the gates of the abbey. All around her, voices stuttered to a halt, and nuns looked at one another with surprised eyes.

The mother abbess closed the Bible, its jeweled cover flashing in the candlelight. "Ellie," she said. "Please go to the gate and find out who needs us at this hour of night."

Ellie nodded and sprang to her feet, then raced into the courtyard, still wet from a summer shower and bathed in late-evening light. Behind the barred iron gate hunched a woman dressed in clothes even rougher than her own, holding a squalling baby tightly to her chest. When she spotted Ellie, she rattled the gate.

"Please, Sister. Oh, please, let me in—the baron and his men, they're after me!"

Ellie's heart gave a sour twist when she looked at the woman's face. She was young, eighteen at the oldest, but so hollowed out with hunger and fear she stood with a grandmother's hunch.

Ellie's own mother had walked straight and proud, until almost the very end. She'd survived Ellie's father leaving them for the Crusade to the Holy Land, from where he'd never returned. She'd lived through the loss of the nice things he'd brought home with him from Nottingham, or built with his own hands—candlesticks, a Bible, their big bed, all of them sold for whatever food Ellie and her mother couldn't grow. Then the baron had gotten wind of their situation. A woman and a child, left unprotected on acres of land they couldn't afford to cultivate. He'd seized their property and evicted them from their home.

Her mother had done what was needed to survive that, too. And then the baron had had his revenge.

*The baron.* He was coming, fast, and Ellie had to hide his quarry before he got there.

She unbarred the gate and hurried the woman into the courtyard. Ellie had to take the baby from her, the woman was shaking so much. The tiny face was hidden by a fold of blanket, and the sour smell of sickness rose from the child's skin. She cradled the poor thing closer, leading the way to the abbey's front hall. There the mother abbess awaited them. Her strong, kind face comforted Ellie immediately—whatever this woman's troubles, the mother abbess would be able to fix them.

"Please," the woman said again, falling on her knees at the abbess's feet.

"There is no need to kneel," the abbess said kindly, helping her up. "Tell me what brings you to our gates."

"It's not for me that I'm here," the woman said, lifting her chin in a threadbare gesture of pride. "It's for him." She nodded at the baby, crying weakly in Ellie's arms. "The baron, he says I owe him taxes—but my husband died a month ago and I've nothing left. Not a penny! The baron says we'll be imprisoned if I can't pay. My son is ill, he won't survive it. If we're put in prison, Reverend Mother, he'll die." She let a sob escape, burying her face in her hands.

Hot rage filled Ellie. What good could it do to imprison a debtor? Would prison cells full of people too sick or too poor to help themselves put more gold into the baron's pockets? And how would they pay him if they *were* free—by selling their cottages, so tumbledown they were barely fit to live in? Or their crops, which didn't produce enough even to feed the people working them?

"Excuse me, Reverend Mother." A purring, unctuous voice came from the corridor just behind the abbess.

Sister Mary Ursula swept forward, moving as though her habit were a ball gown. She had wide, watery blue eyes, and a pinched expression that made it look as if she'd just stepped in dung. She made a performance of moving close to the abbess's ear and then spoke loudly enough for everyone to hear. "My heart goes out to this woman, of course, but we mustn't antagonize the baron. It's only by his leave that we live on his lands. He's well within his rights to arrest this woman. How can we contradict the law? You must refuse sanctuary."

The peasant woman looked down, tears rolling over her cheeks, but the abbess's face remained calm. "Have you considered, Sister Mary Ursula, that we operate by a higher law? She has done little to deserve punishment, and her child nothing at all." The mother abbess smiled at the woman, who instantly smiled back, as if spellbound. "We will offer her the sanctuary she requests—her and any other the baron seeks to persecute."

Sister Mary Ursula only nodded, but Ellie saw her face. It was flushed red, and her eyes narrowed above her permanently pursed mouth.

The abbess guided the peasant woman deeper into the abbey. Ellie's chest was warm with pride as she followed, the baby quieting at last and burrowing against her.

Then a man's gruff voice came through the windows. "Open up, in the name of Lord de Lays!"

From behind the gates came more shouts, and the snorts and whinnies of horses. The peasant woman's eyes widened in terror, and Sister Mary Ursula's head snapped up. She wore a look that said, *I told you how it would be*. It disgusted Ellie.

She pushed the baby gently back into its mother's arms. "The confessional," she said to the mother abbess, who nodded shrewdly.

"Yes," the abbess replied, speaking almost to herself. "God will forgive us for concealing her when a child's safety is at stake." She ushered the pair away.

"Well," said Sister Mary Ursula coldly, watching them go. "Welcome the baron, Elinor. Hurry!"

Ellie bobbed her head and walked as slowly as she dared toward the gate, the small act of defiance putting steel into her spine with every step.

Five men on horseback waited for her—the baron, his constable, and three soldiers. *Five men*, thought Ellie, driving her nails angrily into her palms. *Five men to chase down one starving woman and a sick baby.*

She unbarred the gate and stepped back to let them inside. They glowered down at her, their horses smelling of barnyard and sweat. Ellie stood her ground amid the stamping feet. The soldiers were cloaked in chain mail, swords swinging at their belts. Their faces were lost in shadow beneath their helmets, but Ellie had eyes only for the baron. Four years ago her mother had shot a doe on his land. She and Ellie were starving, sleeping in a neighbor's already-overstuffed cottage, and needed to earn their keep. Needed to *eat*. But her mother was caught, dragged in ropes to the baron's castle. The village was invited to watch as an executioner made Ellie an orphan at the baron's command.

Now she glared up at him, wanting to believe he'd never forgotten her face.

But it seemed he had. "Where is your mother abbess, girl?" he asked in a careless tone, his mount scuffing up mud onto Ellie's habit.

"Good evening, Lord de Lays." The abbess's voice rang out from the doors of the convent. "What brings you to our gates during evening prayers?" She walked toward them, head high, lifting her robes above the muck. Sisters Bethan and Mary Ursula followed in her wake.

"Ah, Reverend Mother." His tone managed to make the title sound lowly. "We're on the trail of a fugitive and have reason to believe that person is being sheltered in the abbey."

Just then, through the colored windows of the chapel, filtered a thin, unmistakable wail. One of the soldiers lifted his chin, as if scenting prey on the air.

Immediately Ellie dropped to the ground. "My foot," she screamed. "His horse—it crushed my foot!"

The horses startled in response to her screams, stamping around Ellie till her foot really was at risk. The baron's horse reared skittishly, and Ellie curled into a ball, praying to God the ruckus would cover the sound of the baby.

The abbess moved into the panting circle of spooked animals and took the baron's mount firmly by the head, whispering at it until it calmed. The baron watched her narrowly.

"Had you a previous life as a horsewoman, Reverend Mother?"

She looked up at him, a flash of steel in her eyes. "A gentle heart can speak to a gentle heart, Baron. All horses are peaceable, when they have a loving master."

Sister Bethan got down on her knees and lifted Ellie's foot gently into her lap. "Only bruised, thanks be to God," she said, then winked so quickly Ellie wasn't sure she'd really seen it. She cried out dramatically as she struggled to her feet, and Sister Bethan gave her a warning squeeze on the shoulder.

"I cannot let you into the abbey." The abbess spoke before the baron could. "If the poor soul you and your men are pursuing were here, he or she would be invoking the legal right of sanctuary. You, Baron, are on dangerous ground, in the eyes of both God and the law. And besides," she added, turning a cool gaze on the other riders, "any fugitive so dangerous as to require five captors could never be contained here. We are defenseless women and would not be so foolish as to let such a monster past our gates."

The baron flushed a funny shade that made Ellie think of undercooked meat. "Sharply done, woman," he said.

Even Sister Mary Ursula stiffened at his disrespect, and Ellie felt her hands ball into fists. The baron wheeled toward the open gate, then looked back at the abbess.

"This isn't the first time a fugitive has gone missing in these parts, Reverend Mother. Do not underestimate me: I know you harbor criminals here, and one day I'll have the means to prove it." With a harsh command toward his men, he led them out the gates.

A brief silence reigned when they were gone. Then the abbess turned briskly, her face cool and calm. "Sister Mary Ursula, our guests need a place to sleep tonight. Please attend to it." The nun bobbed her head grudgingly and walked over the mud toward the abbey doors. "Sister Bethan," the abbess continued, "please bring them something gentle to eat tonight. Porridge, I think." She threw a quick look at Ellie, a glance with something sly in it. "It seems we'll have two more mouths to feed for a time. So a bit of fresh game tomorrow might be nice."

Ellie bit her cheeks to keep from grinning. *So she does know*, she thought, then raced toward the abbey. In the hall she nearly toppled Sister Joan, holding her herb basket and wrapped up tight against the night air.

"Patience is a virtue, Elinor," she said sourly as Ellie retrieved the basket she'd knocked to the floor, then walked as briskly as she dared to her chamber. There she slipped off her plain silver nun's ring and stepped free of the coarse skirts of her habit. Her leggings and hunting tunic felt featherlight in comparison, though Sister Mary Ursula would surely find the leggings to be thoroughly wicked. With that in mind, Ellie moved as stealthily as a cat through the halls, to the kitchen, and out the back door.

Her bow and arrows, retrieved from the ivy, made a comfortable weight on her shoulder. She breathed the air over the garden as she passed—it smelled wet and green. The sun was an orange sliver above the tree line, turning everything it touched into molten gold. Ellie climbed nimbly up the crab apple tree and over the abbey wall. Her feet thumped down on damp grass, and she took off into the beckoning arms of the forest.

# 3

AS SOON AS SHE WAS IN THE TREES, ELLIE FELT lighter. She looked up at the early moon, just a white smudge against the darkening sky, and set her course. A rustling in the underbrush sent her hand reflexively to her bow, but she decided to wait. The hunt was never as satisfying alone. She much preferred the pursuit when she was surrounded by the League of Archers.

When she reached the meeting place, a clearing fringed with berry bushes, the rustling came again, closer. This time she had her bow on her shoulder and an arrow nocked before she could think. *Deer?* she wondered. *Or something bigger?*

It was neither. "Peace, good lady," Jacob Galpin cried,

coming out of the trees with his hands by his ears. "I'm no wolf."

Ellie scowled and whacked him with her bow. "Don't sneak up on me when I'm out for game," she said. "I could've shot you!"

Jacob ducked away, laughing. There was a leaf caught in his short sandy hair, and he was getting so tall she had to crane her neck just to shoot him a dirty look.

"Didn't know if you'd make it tonight," her best friend, Ralf Attwood, said, appearing behind Jacob. He grinned at her from beneath his mop of dark hair. "I'm glad the good mother let you out of your cage."

Ellie grinned when she saw him. She loved the League, but she loved Ralf best of all. When they were kids, they had always fought—over who got to play Robin Hood and who had to be Little John, or who got the bigger piece of honeycomb. But after Ellie's father left for the Holy Land, it was Ralf who took Ellie seriously when she said she wanted to take care of her mother. It was Ralf who helped her make a real bow, before they ever had the guts to go hunting in the woods.

Then, when the baron claimed her family home, it was the Attwoods who took them in. Even as they grieved the death of Ralf's mother, in childbirth with his brother, Henry, they gave the Drays a corner of land to build a cottage on.

The cottage was half-built when Ellie's own mother was hanged. For a while its bones still stood on the Attwoods' land, beams naked against the weather. Then winter came, and they tore it down for firewood. Ellie was glad she didn't have to see it anymore.

Ralf's little sister, Alice, followed him into the clearing now. She was ten years old, skinny as a whip, and tough as horsehide. Ellie could hardly believe she was the same little girl who used to cry when Ralf, three years older, threatened to use her rag doll for target practice.

"Margery's late," Alice said, crossing her arms. "You know that means she'll show up *dripping* in blood."

Now that the older Drubber children were married and keeping their own houses, Margery tended her father's flock by day and helped out in his butcher shop most nights. She was just as likely to cuddle a lamb as slit its throat, depending on the occasion. And because of her, every member of the League of Archers could dress an animal without breaking a sweat.

The League was what they'd called themselves ever since they were little kids, when Ellie's parents were alive and she lived with them in the village. One day, back when she could barely wield the toy bow her father had made her, Ellie, Ralf, and Alice were playing Robin Hood in the woods. They burst into a clearing and found a tiny

Margery standing over Jacob, holding a sharpened stick to his throat—she was playing at being Will Scarlet, and he the Sheriff of Nottingham. After that day they played together.

Until it stopped being a game. They each had their reasons for poaching from the baron, even beyond feeding themselves. Alice always wanted the upper hand. And if she wasn't good at something, she didn't want to do it, so she got good at shooting, fast. Mellow-eyed Jacob was in it for the adventure—his father was a fletcher, making the arrows Jacob stole to supply the League. Men traveled from as far as Nottingham to buy Master Galpin's arrows, so Jacob's family never wanted for food. Margery's family too never lacked for meat. But there was no quest they wouldn't join the others on.

For Ralf it had everything to do with Robin Hood. Robin and his Merry Men had once lived in Sherwood Forest, dashing out to steal from selfish rich men like the baron, then giving their spoils to the peasants starving under King John's rule. The Merry Men had disbanded five years ago, and few had heard of Robin outside of songs and legends since, but he was never far from the people's thoughts. Without his example the League might never have had the courage to slip into the woods to feed themselves. When Ralf went hunting, Ellie knew he was dreaming of a day when he might fight by Robin Hood's side.

But for Ellie, poaching from the baron was personal. She'd seen what he could do, how little he cared about starving families. A few poor harvests and the high taxes to fund King John's war with the French meant most people were only ever a couple of meals away from starving. While the villagers ate gruel as thin as water, the baron and his men hunted for sport, claiming everything that roamed the woods surrounding his castle. With every animal she shot on his lands, she took pleasure in imagining the baron's table getting emptier.

Ellie heard a warning whistle through the trees, and a moment later Margery broke through into the clearing. Her tunic was, indeed, smeared with dried blood, and her messy red hair was swept up under one of her brother's old caps.

"*That's* how you warn someone you're coming," Ellie said, looking pointedly at Jacob. "Especially when that someone could outshoot you with one foot tied to a bucket."

Margery grinned. "Even if you were standing on two buckets, you'd still barely reach his shoulder."

Ralf laughed, and Ellie scoffed, and they were off. The League of Archers, eagle eyed and fleet of foot.

The name had been silly when they took it, five wishful children dreaming of the Merry Men, but now, under the summer starlight, it felt real. In the soft mud beneath an apple tree, where the air was sharp with rotting fruit, Ellie spotted a buck's fragile print. She looked around quickly for the trail of broken branches that might mark the animal's path.

When the League took down a deer for the first time, it was Ellie who made the killing shot. After that the rest of the League started looking to her first. She'd been the leader then, even though Ralf was a year older and Jacob the same age as her, and she was the leader now. Nothing could change that, not even being sent to live at the abbey.

The bow she held wasn't her first—that one had been taken by the baron. Her mother had used it to make the kill that became her death sentence, and the baron kept it as evidence. Every time Ellie remembered it, the misery twisted her stomach like she'd eaten a fistful of poisonous berries.

After Ellie's mother was hanged, and knowing Master Attwood was already struggling to feed his own children, the mother abbess came to take Ellie away. Weak with a grief that felt like sickness, Ellie hadn't fought it. But the night before she went, the League gathered together in the Attwoods' yard. Ralf coaxed Ellie out into the moonlight. They hugged her good-bye and swore they'd stick together. Ralf pressed the new bow he'd made into her hands, and curled her fingers around it. "You're our leader no matter what," he told her. "You'll just have to find a way to sneak out of the abbey."

So she did. And now she could sense her friends following close behind as they stalked their target. Ellie saw the buck through the trees and raised a hand for quiet. The moon was up, painting the animal's flank a silvery gray. Too soon Alice lifted her bow to her shoulder and shot—she was always too impatient, too eager to prove herself. Her arrow lodged itself into a tree just over the buck's head. With a liquid leap he was out of sight.

"Stupid bow," Alice said, glaring mutinously at it.

"Why'd you do that? You didn't have close to a clear shot!" said Ralf, irritated.

"No need to scold her," said Margery peaceably. "She'll do enough of that to herself."

Ellie peered longingly at the buck's broken path, then saw something that made her blood chill. A figure in a dark cloak, moving quick as a thief between two trees. *The baron's gamekeeper.*

"Hide yourselves, now," she said in a hoarse whisper. The League had been following her long enough, had their skins saved by her quick thinking often enough, that they slid behind trees and into bushes without question, as quietly as if they were wild creatures themselves. Ellie folded herself into a crouch behind the twisting trunk of a hazel tree, pressing a hand against its bark for comfort.

She spent a long minute listening to her speeding heart slow to normal, craning to hear the approaching gamekeeper. When nothing happened, she stood and gave a two-tone whistle. The League emerged from their hiding spots, Jacob rubbing a new bee sting on his hand. "Shouldn't have hidden in honeysuckle," he said ruefully.

"I really thought I saw the gamekeeper," Ellie said. "Just imagined it, I suppose." And maybe she had. The figure had been distant enough that she wasn't sure.

They set off again through the trees, more subdued this time. As they walked, Ellie told them about the woman taking sanctuary in the abbey. They all went quiet for a moment, remembering what the baron had done to Ellie's mother.

"If Robin Hood were still around, this would be just the kind of thing he'd put a stop to," Ralf said darkly.

Alice scoffed. "If Robin Hood were still around, we'd know about it. Or *someone* would. And besides, what could he do about the baron? Kill him?"

"There's a thought," Jacob said, parrying an invisible foe. "He'd take him on in hand-to-hand combat, and the baron would trip over his own fancy cloak."

Ellie shook her head. "Things are worse than they were before," she said. "The abbey can't keep up with what's needed. No matter what we do, there are people going hungry. Dying of it." She thought of the starving boy in the abbey hospital, the way his face lit up when she told him the story about the silver arrow. "When Robin Hood was around, he was like a warning for wicked men. He scared them just enough to make them . . . not kinder . . . just more careful." She looked at Alice, the smallest and most stubborn among them. "You're too young to remember when Robin came to our village and gave us food. But we would have died without him."

That was just after Ellie's father left, but before the baron drove them out of Dray House. Her mother stopped smiling that winter. Her face grew as still and cold as the frozen surface of the pond as their storehouse grew emptier.

Then Robin came. Ellie still remembered his lean, frostbitten face, the kind blue eyes that twinkled at her when he gave her grateful mother a side of venison, bags of grain, enough supplies to get them through the winter. Her mother seemed to wake up after that, to remember she and Ellie were a family even if her husband never came back. It was after that night that Ellie and her friends started calling themselves the League of Archers.

"But he could've been anyone," Alice argued. "Any outlaw with a mind to break the law."

"That's the whole point," said Margery. "Robin Hood showed us that anybody—a *nobody*—could be brave enough to fight back."

"But it couldn't have been just any outlaw," Ralf insisted. "Robin Hood, he's faster than other men, strong. He's braver, too. And just *better*." He flushed, hearing himself, but Jacob nodded.

"My dad gave him a clutch of his best arrows for free that winter," he said. "For him and the Merry Men. I hope they caught a whole flock of barons with them."

"I love the idea of Robin Hood as much as anyone," Ellie said slowly, "but I think Margery's right. The outlaw who saved us that winter could've been another man borrowing Robin's name, and it would've been just as good." Her mind was sparking with something, half a thought. "It's not the man that's important, it's what he stands for."

"You're all talking nonsense," Alice said. "Robin was just a man. A man who did good things once, then stopped."

Jacob grinned. "Well, let's honor his memory. We'll steal some game from the rich and give it to the poor." He rubbed his belly. Ralf groaned and shoved his shoulder.

Then a flickering movement in the trees caught Ellie's eye—the buck was back, or one of his brothers. His neck made a graceful curve as he scented something on the wind. As one, they shouldered their bows.

"On my signal," Ellie said through her teeth. Her bow was taut in her hand. The buck froze in place, sensing something amiss.

"*Now.*"

Five arrows flew toward the animal; two found their mark. Ellie let out a breath when hers hit his eye. Instantly the creature staggered, then fell.

When they reached the downed buck, the hot haze of his final breaths hung around him, but his chest was still. As always when they made a kill, Ellie thought of her mother. She was certain that despite the danger, despite the risk, her mother would be proud of her now.

The buck's gaze was dull, but they hung back a moment to make sure he was gone. Back when they were green hunters, Ralf had taken a kick to the ribs from a dying doe.

"Dead," Margery said cheerfully. "Good shot, Ellie." She crouched between the animal's forelegs and pulled out her knife. Ellie kept her gaze on the trees over Margery's head, scanning them for any sign of movement—and keeping the butchering at the edge of her sight. She wasn't squeamish about doing what it took to stay alive, but she still didn't love the gutting.

Jacob unpacked rolls of clean cloth from his knapsack, taken from among his mother's midwifing supplies. Margery divided their shares, with extra for Ellie to take back to the abbey. Ellie regretted having to leave the skin and bones behind—perfect for clothing and soup—but they could take only what they could carry.

"You know what the League needs," Ralf said, hefting his share and part of Alice's over his shoulder. "Our own Little John. He was even taller than Jacob—seven feet!"

"Or a cart," Alice pointed out. "Nobody needs a giant for a best friend when they've got a perfectly good cart."

While Margery worked, Ellie gathered green branches to cover the remains of the deer. She sprinkled the lot with honeysuckle blossoms in hopes of covering the scent.

A dog barked. Too close. No amount of honeysuckle would be enough. Dread made her stomach clench—the gamekeeper was on their trail. "Quick," she said, snatching up her own bundle. "Run!"

# 4

THE FOREST FLASHED AROUND THEM IN DIM shades of gray and white. Ellie's heart was beating so hard it almost drowned out their steps—almost. Five sets of feet couldn't be silent, no matter how well trained, and every crackling branch or crash through the dark undergrowth made her more certain the gamekeeper would catch up.

Then she smelled something, a fresh mossy scent—the stream just a quarter mile away.

She whistled and changed course, throwing a glance over her shoulder to make sure they stayed together. Margery's eyes shone white in the moonlight, and Alice's face was set with fear. The trees thinned out around them, until they were half sliding down a long, muddy bank. Small nocturnal creatures darted clear of their path, and a fox let out an indignant bark when Ellie nearly collided with it as she rounded an elm tree. Finally they reached the stretch of rushes that led to open water. Ellie plunged into the muck, turning only when Alice yelped and let out an astonishing stream of whispered curses. Already she was struggling to her feet, having fallen face-first into the mud.

"Come *on*," Ellie whispered as Ralf pulled Alice the rest of the way up.

The gamekeeper's dog bayed behind them, too close. Reeds slapped Ellie in the face as she plunged desperately toward the stream.

Finally she broke through into clear, cold water. In a few paces she was in up to her knees. Dimly she could see a great tumble of boulders forming a sort of cave just upstream, and she told her quivering legs to keep going long enough to get her there.

"Ralf, Jacob, stay by Margery," Ellie called over her shoulder as loudly as she dared. "I think we can get to those rocks without going over our heads." All of them could swim except Margery, who always sank like a stone no matter how many summers they spent trying to teach her.

Alice plunged in and paddled, and the rest of them

splashed clumsily toward the shelter. Ellie prayed the rushing of the stream would cover the sound.

Finally they were there, pulling themselves into the space between two lichen-covered stones. No sooner were they hidden than the gamekeeper crashed through the trees— Ellie guessed he'd wasted time avoiding the marshy stretch of land. His dog barked across the water. Its echoing snarls made Ellie's fingers squeeze tight around Margery's.

"I know you're there," the gamekeeper growled. His voice was even worse than the dog's, as black and broken as his teeth.

"We're done for," whispered Ralf, his voice hoarse with fear.

Ellie held up a hand to quiet him and watched through a gap in the rocks. The dog sniffed the ground, then raised its nose to the air, tossing its head. Through the gloom Ellie saw the man's head turn back and forth, surveying the dark bank opposite him.

"No," Ellie whispered. "They've lost our scent."

Man and hound paced on the shore a minute longer, until the animal finally skittered back. After another long minute the gamekeeper turned. "Come on, boy," he muttered. "I ain't risking a chill for the baron. There's a fire back at the lodge. And ale." The two went back into the woods, their footfalls fading into the distance.

Ellie's breath whooshed out of her, spots swimming before her eyes. Margery let out a stunned laugh, as she always did when scared or relieved or even angry, and Jacob put a hand to his heart. "I thought we were dinner for the dog," he said dramatically.

"That dog could do better than us, I'm sure," Ellie replied. "We're far too scrawny." Her voice was almost as steady as she willed it to be. "Come on." She led them back, clasping the slippery rocks and pulling herself through the rippling water.

Ralf looked glum as they trailed onto the bank. "Of all the nights to waste our time running like rabbits," he said. "I thought we'd catch another deer at least."

Ellie eyed the sizable bundle on his back, and the smaller one on Alice's. "We'll hunt again as soon as we can. Won't that be enough to keep you?"

Ralf just shook his head, his jaw set, and Alice sighed. "The baron's tax collectors have found themselves even bigger pockets," she said wearily. "Father had to give away half our grain just to get them away from the door."

"Little do they know I mixed rat droppings in, as a treat," Ralf joked. Alice smiled at her brother, but Ellie could see it was a struggle.

She shifted her own pack of meat, thinking of the warm abbey kitchen, where Sister Bethan would turn it into a delicious stew, then stretch out the rest so it flavored their dishes for a week. She saw the faces of the patients in the hospital, and their starving stomachs as tight as the baron's fist.

But the abbey had gardens and goats, and trees heavy with fruit. Ellie swung the meat off her shoulder and pushed it into Alice's hands, stepping back before she could refuse it.

"For the little ones," she said, thinking of the two Attwoods even younger than Alice, their faces always thinner than they should be. "Just make sure Matilda eats her share." Matilda Attwood fussed over Henry, the baby of the family, like a little mother; if she had her way, he'd eat the food off her own plate.

"I'll shoot some ducks for the abbey on the way back." She affected a fancy accent. "Though it won't be *near* so nice as what Sister Mary Ursula is used to." Her friends' laughter gave her a feeling more satisfying than stew.

Alice just nodded her thanks, pride keeping her from speaking, but Ralf threw an arm around Ellie's shoulders. "We thank you, and all the sisters who will have to make do with porridge," he said half seriously.

They clasped hands all around, grinning at the old ritual, and made plans to meet again in a few days. "Unless my sister's baby comes then," Margery said, frowning.

"The only thing in the world that turns my stomach, but I'm expected to help with the birth anyway."

Margery had more nieces and nephews than Ellie could count. It gave her a twinge to think of a warm house full of family, so many you could never run out. She kissed Margery on the cheek and smiled. "That's for the baby, when it comes," she said.

Their wild flight from the gamekeeper had taken her far from home, but she took her time walking back, hoping to spot something tastier than the mangy, quarrelsome ducks that paddled through the pond near the abbey. A fat rabbit, perhaps.

But there were no rabbits to be seen as Ellie stalked through the forest.

*Duck it is*, she thought, and turned toward the pond. Moonlight washed through the thinning canopy above her and danced on the water, where a mallard paddled in the shallows. It was a tricky shot, half-obscured by reeds, but she knew the duck might flap off if she tried to get too close.

"At least you'll taste better than porridge," she muttered, sighting down her arrow. She breathed in— then the unmistakable *whoosh-snap* of an arrow leaving a bow broke her concentration.

Not her arrow. Not her bow. But it flew truly and hit the duck, killing it in one clean shot. Ellie gaped—she could hit a stag's eye, but not a *duck's*. She turned, looking around wildly for the archer.

A man stood behind her, too close. A hood covered his eyes in shadow, but she saw a cropped gray beard and the smile it almost hid. His bow was better than hers, she could tell that at a glance. It was made of something fine and flexible that made her fingers itch with wanting.

She saw all this in half a moment, then turned, prepared to flee.

"Wait!" he said, and his voice was so full of good humor that she stayed. "I'm not looking for trouble, just something for my supper. I see now I may have chosen your duck."

"*Your* duck," she said, turning slowly. "You shot first." She studied what part of his face she could see, wondering what it was about him that put her so at ease. "A good shot, too."

"You can have its brother," he said, pointing toward a second duck paddling across the water. "The foolish thing doesn't have the sense to fly away."

Ellie turned and lifted her bow to her shoulder. She tried to ignore the feeling of eyes on her back, and the sense she had something to prove by making this shot. Unless—what if this was one of the baron's men, trying to goad her into poaching right in front of him? She rejected the thought. Whoever this man was, he was no servant.

She aimed at the duck—then another arrow whooshed past her, making another perfect kill.

The man laughed quietly, and she spun around with her fists clenched. "What do you think you're doing?" she spat. "That was my duck."

"Not by your accounting—I shot first. Again. And I might just as easily ask what *you're* doing. A young girl out shooting ducks in the moonlight, all on her own."

Ellie bristled. "I have mouths to feed, sir, not just my own. And I'm taking one of those ducks whether I shot it or not."

The man was silent as she waded into the pond—*Oh well*, she thought, *my clothes were soaked anyway*—to retrieve the bobbing ducks. When she reached land again, he hadn't moved. She dropped one duck at his feet and shouldered the other.

"I hope your hungry mouths are grateful," he said kindly. "It's a noble thing you do, helping those who can't help themselves."

The shift in his voice kept Ellie from walking away, even though the moon was starting to climb back down the sky and the thought of her bed was more tempting every minute. "You think so?" she said tentatively.

"There are two choices only that a man can make," he said, not seeming to realize he was changing the subject.

"Or a girl, of course. To shut your eyes and help only yourself, or to keep them open and shoulder the needs of the world. But whether it's one duck or ten ducks or a thousand ducks, it's never enough." His eyes were still hooded, but his gaze seemed to be focused somewhere over Ellie's head. "There aren't enough arrows in this world to turn the tide," he said.

"The tide?" she echoed faintly.

He started, as if he'd forgotten she was there, then smiled and leaned down to pick up his duck. "I'm an old man rambling," he said. "But I'd love to see what you can do with that bow. Try it again on that rabbit just there, and this time I won't show off."

His words filled Ellie with a quicksilver feeling. Her bow felt light in her hand, like an extension of her arm. "I bet I can kill it in one, same as you," she said—then an arrow whizzed past her shoulder again, so close she felt the quick breeze of it. But this time it came from the dark woods at her back.

Almost as soon as it passed, the man's mouth went slack. In the sudden clarity of shock Ellie saw the bright red of the arrow's fletching, and the way it pierced the stranger's shoulder like a knife through meat. A bloom of dark blood spread across his cloak as he dropped to his knees.

He'd been shot.

# 5

ELLIE SPUN AROUND, HER HEART IN HER THROAT
and an arrow on her bowstring. Something moved at the
edge of the tree line, and she let her arrow fly—clumsily.
It disappeared into the dark. She nocked another arrow
and ran forward a few paces, eyes narrowed. But whoever
had been watching them was gone.

She turned her attention back toward the injured
man. His eyes were wide and his fingers moved weakly
by his shoulder, as if to pull out the arrow himself. The
blood pumping from his wound dyed his tunic dark as
Communion wine.

"Don't. I'll do it." Ellie tried to channel Margery's
brusque calm. What would Sister Joan tell her to do? She

ripped the man's tunic free from his wound. The arrow was lodged in the meat just under his arm, deeply but well clear of his heart. She let her breath out in a whoosh. If she worked fast, it shouldn't be fatal.

"Try not to move," Ellie said grimly. She wrapped both hands around the arrow, gave the man a tiny nod, then pulled it straight upward. It slid free with a sickly suck. She threw it to the ground, fighting to keep her voice steady as the blood came fast and dark. "Here, keep pressure on the wound with your other hand. Now stand up and rest your weight on me."

"Don't forget . . . the ducks," he panted.

Ellie blinked, wondering if he was raving. "We'll leave them for some other hunter. I need to get you indoors."

His eyes widened. "Where?" It was all he could get out before a wave of pain made him squeeze his eyes shut.

"Kirklees Abbey is just beyond that rise," she said, pointing. "I'm a novice there. The abbess will help us."

His eyes snapped open and locked on hers. "Kirklees," he said, his voice thick and strange. "You come from Kirklees Abbey?" The man rose shakily to his feet, staggered a moment, and leaned heavily against Ellie.

Beneath the heavy, metallic tang of blood he smelled like woodsmoke and forest. "There you are, then," Ellie babbled, trying to push down her own fear. "That's not so bad, is it?"

"I've had worse wounds than this," he said. But his smile turned into a grimace, and he seemed to grow weaker with every step. It was hard going up the slight hill to the abbey, and even harder going down, with the tilt of the earth threatening to make them tumble.

Ellie moved doggedly forward, until sweat soaked through her clothes and her whole body quivered with the strain. The man seemed less and less able to carry his own weight. When the abbey came into sight, Ellie sneaked a glance at his wound, stifling a gasp. Under the blood the man's shoulder had swollen up like bread dough, to double its size. How could that be?

When they finally reached the abbey's gates, Ellie tugged desperately on the bell. The man still stood upright, but his eyes were closed, and his cheeks looked grayish in the moonlight.

"Almost there," she whispered, fearing he was too far gone to hear. The relief she felt when someone moved in the blackness beyond the gate was only partially quenched when she saw who it was: Sister Mary Ursula, with two older sisters named Margaret and Hilda, and a nightgowned Agnes, trailing in her wake.

Mary Ursula's thin face wore a look of sour victory.

"It's nearly dawn, girl. This is the gratitude you show to the mother abbess for taking you in?" She stopped only when Agnes touched her arm.

"Please, Sister," she said. "The man is badly wounded."

They moved to open the gate, and Ellie's strength finally gave out. She lowered the man to the ground as gently as she could. Slits of white shone beneath his eyelids, and his mouth moved as though he were trying to speak. Sister Mary Ursula watched stonily, hands clasped, as Agnes and the other nuns helped Ellie lift him again and carry him across the yard and into the abbey.

The mother abbess appeared just beyond the doorway, her expression stern in the light of the candle she held aloft. "I'll wake Sister Joan," she said, "and let her know she's needed in the hospital." Then she angled her candle to illuminate the man's sweat-streaked face, and a change came over her.

"Where did you—how did you—how badly is he hurt?" Her voice was broken, her face suddenly distraught. "Never mind," she said, regaining some of her composure. "Bring him to my room."

Ellie wondered for a moment if she'd misunderstood. Bring a bleeding man to the abbess's own chambers? She herself had never been past the doorway.

"To your room?" Sister Mary Ursula repeated, her voice edged in horror. "Surely you cannot . . . We have beds in the hospital, Reverend Mother. This man, this . . . *peasant* is covered in blood and filth! He was likely injured in a bar brawl, and now takes advantage of your kindness."

The mother abbess ignored her, moving to the man's head. She cradled it in her free hand as they moved him down the hall, continuing past the hospital wing. By the time they laid him across the abbess's narrow bed, his mouth was no longer moving.

"Sister Mary Ursula, bring hot water and clean cloths," the abbess said. "Elinor, light those candles. Every one. The rest of you, go back to your rooms and try to sleep. And remember the virtue of discretion."

Ellie took the candle from the abbess's shaking hand and used it to light the others on the sill of her open window, and those lined up on the heavy wooden chest carved with pomegranates that stood next to her bed. Behind her the man groaned.

But who was he? More than just a stranger she met in the woods, surely, if he provoked this change in the mother abbess. After Ellie lit the last candle, she turned to see the abbess bending over the man to examine his wound.

Then the abbess drew in a breath and pressed her

LEAGUE OF ARCHERS

hands to her eyes. When she spoke, her voice was heavy with sorrow. "The wound is poisoned," she said. "There is no hope."

"Poisoned?" Ellie echoed faintly. The puncture looked worse than ever, the skin around it bubbling like fat atop a pot of soup.

The man's eyelids fluttered, and he took in a gasping breath. "Marian," he breathed. "Marian."

*Calling for his wife*, Ellie thought, her heart squeezing with pity. Then she saw the abbess's face. Her blue eyes were tear filled, trained on the man's, and her smile was sad and tender.

"Oh, Robin," she said. She held one hand to his heart and cupped the other around his face.

And it struck Ellie like summer lightning. The man's unnatural skill with a bow, his strange ramblings in the woods. The name he'd called out—the mother abbess's name. *Marian.*

She was Maid Marian. And this man was Robin Hood.

Ellie felt hot and cold all at once, sudden grief warring with a burning curiosity. Maid Marian a nun? Robin Hood a lonely hunter? What could've happened that led them to this?

Before Ellie could speak, Sister Mary Ursula was back, holding a bowl of steaming water and an armful of rough cloth. But the abbess had eyes only for the wounded man. "How did this happen, Robin?" she asked.

He moved his fingers weakly, twining them around hers. "We always knew, Marian," he whispered. "We always knew I wouldn't die of old age."

Sister Mary Ursula blinked at the scene and then edged backward from the room, leaving the supplies behind. Ellie thought, dimly, that she should leave too, but couldn't tear herself from the sight of the abbess and the archer, clasping hands in the candlelight.

"*You* always knew," the abbess said. "But I always hoped."

Robin smiled, with effort. "I never deserved it. I never deserved you. I told you that."

"You also told me to forget you. You said I could if I tried. You were wrong about that, too."

He shook his head. "No, Marian. After what I did . . . I didn't deserve happiness."

"If you'd just tell me what it was—if you could just explain . . . Give me peace, Robin." The abbess's voice crackled with sorrow and something else, an old anger.

"No, Marian. I like to see your eyes like this," he whispered. "Like you love me still. The things I've done can't be forgiven."

The abbess kissed him, on the mouth, then both cheeks.

Their tears ran together and shone in the candlelight. Ellie watched them through the mist of her own, trying to make herself small against the wall.

Robin moaned again and closed his eyes. Ellie saw fear in the abbess's face—the fear that he wouldn't speak again.

But he did. "Put them in my hands," he said. "My bow. And my quiver."

They had been dropped on the ground with his bloody, shredded tunic. Ellie rushed to gather them up and give them to the abbess. She took them reverently and gave them to him.

By touch he selected an arrow from within the quiver. It was unlike its brothers: slender, made of silver that glowed in the early light coming through the window.

Ellie's gasped as she recognized it: the silver arrow from the archery contest, given to him by the Sheriff of Nottingham. It made everything sharper and more real. This was Robin Hood, the outlaw and the legend. And his life was slipping away before her eyes.

Holding the arrow in one hand, Robin hoisted himself to a sitting position. The abbess stepped back, her chin lifting proudly. With fluid grace and an unexpected strength, he brought the bow to his shoulder, and the arrow to the bow.

He turned toward the window, sighting down the

glinting arrow. Ellie drank up the sight hungrily, knowing in her heart that she and Maid Marian would be the last to see the great Robin Hood shoot.

Then he let loose the silver arrow. It flew in a singing straight line, cutting the dawn in two and disappearing from sight.

He dropped weakly back onto the bed and turned his head toward the abbess.

"Marian," he said again. His voice brimmed with something that made Ellie's heart ache. "Bury me where it falls."

As the air outside slowly lightened, into a morning Robin Hood wouldn't live to see, a shudder passed through his body. Then he went still.

It was a long moment before Ellie could look away, before her mind could catch up to her broken heart. Robin Hood was dead. She had finally met him, only to see him killed by an assassin's hand.

The abbess's head was bowed, her usually placid gaze stricken with grief. She held her jeweled Bible tightly in her hands, hovering over Robin's body, but didn't open it to read a prayer. Instead she just clutched it, the way Ellie had clutched her rag doll in the days after her mother's hanging.

When the first wave of horror had passed, Ellie's mind

began to race. Who could have done this? And why? Ralf's face swam before her eyes, lit with admiration for Robin Hood. How bitter would he be to know his hero was dead? And what of the people in their village? Every child heard bedtime stories of Robin's bravery. How could they bear to know he had died this way—not in battle, but from a cowardly assassin's arrow?

A sudden commotion carried through the window— the sound of approaching horses and, worse, men's voices. The abbess still hovered by Robin's side, but Ellie rushed to the window.

Men on horseback filled the yard. She counted seven and remembered with sharp regret that she and the sisters had left the gate unlocked. She barely had time to register the footsteps outside the abbess's chambers before the door burst open.

The baron stood in front of another man Ellie recognized from darker times: the constable, as fat and comfortable as Robin was ragged and thin. Behind them was a trio of armed guards—and Sister Mary Ursula. Her eyes shone with suppressed triumph, but the baron didn't even try to hide his emotion. An ugly grin spread across his face.

"Maid Marian," he said. "I have you at last."

# 6

THE ABBESS STRAIGHTENED UP, HER FACE
hardening into an expression of distant politeness. It was
the bravest thing Ellie had ever seen.

The baron stepped closer, eyes victorious. "I never
would've believed it," he marveled. "You were pretty
once, they say. Now that I know, I can see it in your face.
The same arrogance she always had—that *you* always had."

"I told you she was dangerous, Baron," Sister Mary
Ursula babbled. "Only you and I saw her for what she truly
was, all these years. Worse than a wolf in sheep's clothing—a
criminal wearing the guise of a woman of God!"

"And I've caught you," the baron said, ignoring
Sister Mary Ursula. "All this time I've suspected you of

harboring fugitives, and now I learn you're a fugitive yourself—and harboring the Crown's greatest enemy!"

Still the abbess remained silent, her eyes on the baron's. She didn't look once at the constable or the guards.

"Well, woman, what do you say to these charges?" The baron's face grew red—the abbess clearly wasn't the sniveling quarry he was hoping for. "Here lies the great outlaw Robin Hood, dead on my lands—and here are you, caught in the act of protecting him! What do you say?"

"That I think you must be very proud," the abbess replied coolly. "Like all truly great men, you dare to face your enemy the moment he's dead, and use a nun to do your spying."

Ellie's heart surged with glee and terror in equal measure. For a moment she feared the baron might actually hit the abbess. Perhaps it was years of seeing her as the mother abbess that stayed his hand.

Through gritted teeth he spoke. "Is it sheer arrogance that drives you, woman, or utter disdain for your God and your king? By what machinations did you ever convince the church to take you in?"

"The church will always provide sanctuary for those who need it," Marian said. "As Sister Mary Ursula can attest."

The nun's nostrils flared at the sound of her name, her eyes narrowing to slits. "Don't compare yourself to me, sinner," she hissed. "I was the daughter of a lord. You were the kept woman of an outlaw!"

"My father was as rich as yours, Sister," the abbess replied, "and my husband would've been richer, if I'd accepted him. To answer your question, Baron, I entered the abbey to escape a forced marriage. To the Sheriff of Nottingham."

The baron cocked his head in disbelief. "That man escaped a fate worse than—"

"You prideful thing," Sister Mary Ursula broke in, her voice shaking. "Too good for the life he could've given you . . . too good for silks and jewels?" Her thin face was ugly with jealousy.

"Too good to be the property of a man I hated," Marian snapped. It was the first time Ellie had heard her lose her temper. "Kirklees gave me independence. It gave me a home and food and comfort. And sisters. Just as it did you. I'm not the one with a prideful heart, Mary Ursula."

Sister Mary Ursula reared back, as if to spit in Marian's face, and the constable let out an eager half laugh. "Perhaps this one can do my job for me," he said. "Shall we let her take the outlaw off our hands?"

"Don't be a fool," the baron replied harshly. "The lady is my prisoner. I hereby arrest you, Maid Marian, for the crime of harboring a dangerous fugitive from the king's justice, and for your own crimes of outlawry."

"And I, I will give evidence," Sister Mary Ursula put in, getting some of her composure back. "Too long have I fought against her disdain for the Crown. I have witnessed too much to remain silent!"

Again the baron ignored her; he had eyes only for the abbess. "You've been an enemy to my rule and to common decency for years, but this time, Maid Marian, you'll hang."

It was too much for Ellie. "You can't do this!" she broke in. The men's surprise when she spoke told her they'd taken no more notice of her than they would a Bible or a chair. "You've broken every rule of the church—you've violated the right of sanctuary!" Her voice shook, but she spoke as loudly as she could.

"She's right," growled a voice from the doorway. Sister Bethan, with a knot of nuns behind her. She gave Ellie a nod, her eyes fierce. "You've violated a godly place and are now threatening to take our mother abbess away without cause or evidence."

The baron pointed at Robin's cold form. "I call this evidence. Now all of you, get out of my way or pay the price." He waved his hand at the men around him, and with a loathsome *snick* they drew their swords.

"Swords?" Sister Bethan was so angry she could barely speak. "On unarmed brides of Christ and a girl-child?"

"Stop, Sister Bethan, I beg of you." The abbess's voice was quiet. "We've long known this man here has no respect for the laws of God, or the rights of men. Let them pass. I won't have anyone hurt on my account."

One of the guards grabbed the abbess's arm and wrenched it behind her back. At her wince of pain Ellie launched herself forward, pulling uselessly at the man's hands.

"Let go—you're hurting her!"

In the next moment she was lifted off her feet. The constable's breath washed over her, smelling of boiled cabbage. She heard Sister Bethan scream as he pressed the flat of a knife to Ellie's throat. "God made us men in his image, girl," he said. "You should show your betters a mite more respect."

The blade was cool against her skin. Ellie watched helplessly as the abbess was taken roughly from the room. Sister Bethan tried to follow after her but was blocked by a guard.

"I'm sorry, Sister." His voice was low and touched with shame. "She's the king's prisoner now."

"You two get the body," the baron said, pointing

**LEAGUE OF ARCHERS**

toward Robin. "And don't forget his bow. The king will reward me handsomely for this quarry."

The constable spoke again, his chest rumbling against Ellie's back. "The king will thank you for it, to be sure, but the peasants will cry out for blood. Do you really think they'll believe Robin Hood was so obliging as to be killed in your backyard? They might just as easily think you did it." His tone was pleasant, speculative. "I shouldn't be surprised if they riot, burn a few of their hovels. I might even put a wager on revolt."

The baron nodded slowly. Ellie could practically see the wheels ticking dully into motion in his mind. "A revolt. The king wouldn't thank me for *that*."

"If I may, Lord de Lays, perhaps what you need is a scapegoat." Ellie could swear Sister Mary Ursula's voice sounded a hundred times more pinched and aristocratic than it had the last time she spoke. "Such simpleminded folk can keep only one idea in their heads at once. All they need is someone to hate—someone to *blame*."

Sister Bethan drew in a sharp breath. "Mary Ursula, you hold your vile tongue."

The sister ignored her. "And it just so happens we have a very proficient archer on our hands," she continued silkily. "The very person who brought the dying outlaw to our gates—Novice Elinor Dray."

A cold, distant feeling came over Ellie as the baron looked at her appraisingly. She felt as if she were watching this unfold from a mile away. Then a sly smile split his face, and she crashed back into herself, struggling against the constable's thick arm.

"What, this knee-high chit?" the constable was saying doubtfully, but the baron moved forward to grab Ellie's hand in his clammy one, pumping it twice as if they'd just made a devil's deal.

"Yes, you'll do, you insolent brat. Congratulations on the one great thing you'll ever do: killing that infamous outlaw, Robin Hood!"

"I would never!" Ellie gasped, still fighting to escape the constable's iron grasp. "It must've been you—you set an assassin on him, and now you're leaving me the blame!"

As she said the words, the rightness of them hit her. Who else could be responsible for the mysterious archer and his poisoned arrow? But the baron just laughed with dark delight.

"I won't lie to you, my dear, I wish I had—but it was *you* who loosed the fatal arrow!"

"They'll never believe you," she said with more confidence than she felt. "Nobody will ever believe you!"

His eyes narrowed. "Oh, but they will. You think I've forgotten you, girl?"

Ellie's blood chilled as he surveyed her face. *So he does remember.*

"The grubby child of that lawless woman who stole from my land. You passed from her care into the hands of Maid Marian—the worst woman ever to pollute Sherwood Forest. Two criminals have raised a third. Your mother swung for her crimes, but you—you shall be rewarded."

"No," Sister Bethan said desperately, breaking free of the guard. "She's just a child. Please, see reason!"

The baron ignored her. "Escort Novice Dray to my castle. She'll spend the night there, as my honored guest."

"Your guest or your prisoner?" Ellie's voice scraped over her dry throat.

"Don't worry, child." His smile made her stomach twist. "I'm going to give you the reward you deserve."

The constable marched her through the abbey and out its front doors. As he pushed her into the yard, she wished desperately for her tiny cell and her narrow bed. Kirklees had been her home for four years. If the baron carried her away, she feared she would never see it again.

The muddy yard was full of nuns, their faces angry and fearful in the washed blue light of early morning. Ellie's heart ached to see them, knowing she wouldn't wake up to pray with them tomorrow morning. She wouldn't see Sister Bethan wink as she poured an extra ladle of stew into her bowl. She wouldn't see the neat braids of the littlest novices, plaited tightly by Agnes's clever hands. Sister Joan wouldn't be there to sigh with mixed irritation and affection when Ellie forgot what exactly went into a tincture for headache.

The nuns clustered around Maid Marian, who sat upright on a horse's saddle with her hands bound in front of her. The soldier at her back made no effort to keep a respectful distance from her body. Sister Ethel stood as close as she could, twisting her hands into her skirt. She looked as if she wished she were twisting them around the guard's throat instead.

Agnes gasped and started to cry when she saw Ellie held by her captor, but Ellie looked only to Marian. The expression in her eyes made Ellie's heart plummet. Inside, the abbess had still seemed defiant. Now she just looked lost and heartbroken.

The baron strode into the yard, his long face victorious.

"For years you have labored under the delusion that your mother abbess is a godly woman. But today she has shown her true colors!"

The nuns looked from him to the mother abbess.

"She is no abbess," he continued. "She is Maid Marian, a wanted criminal. And thanks to me, the king will have his justice against her at last."

In the sea of shocked faces Ellie saw one that was not—
Sister Bethan's. *She knew,* Ellie thought, *and she kept Maid
Marian's secret.* The thought of the nun's loyalty put a small,
quiet flame of courage into her own heart.

But the baron's next words snuffed it out. "Only one of
you had the fortitude to report my prisoner's misdeeds—
Sister Mary Ursula. I thereby name her your new mother
abbess."

Sister Mary Ursula lifted her head higher, like a wolf
smelling prey on the air. A thin, greedy smile broke over
her face as she smoothed her hands down the coarse
front of her nightgown. Sister Bethan looked as if she
could spit poison, and Agnes was pale as milk. Some of
the other sisters seemed unsure, but most looked stricken
or worse. Their voices combined into a furious rumble,
and Ellie added her own to the crowd's. "But you can't
do that!" she cried.

The constable's voice was amused, and close to her
ear. "You have much to say on what the baron cannot
do," he said. "You'd do well to learn quickly how very
wrong you are."

# 7

ELLIE RODE WITH THE CONSTABLE. THE ONLY
horses she'd ever been on were an ancient nag belonging
to Margery's family and, long ago, her own father's
plodding mare. Her first ride on a real horse—a freckled,
spirited animal who seemed much kinder than his
master—should have been thrilling. Instead she spent
it recoiling from the constable's grasp and peering into
the trees lining the narrow road. She imagined Ralf or
Alice peeking out at her from the leaves. They'd fire
their arrows into the baron and his men, before leading
Ellie and the abbess into the forest. There they'd reunite
with the Merry Men and avenge Robin Hood's death.
But all she saw were crowds of starlings swooping over

the brightening sky, and once a roe deer standing frozen between two trunks. She watched him for a heartbeat before the horse carried her away.

She'd seen the baron's castle only from afar, from the village that pooled in the shallow valley below. As they broke free of the trees, she saw it crouched on the land like an ugly animal, circled by high walls and a deep moat.

It grew larger with every moment, until they came to a stamping halt outside its walls, which rose far over the horses' heads, gray stone furred over with moss. The baron shouted a greeting to the guards manning the bridge, who stepped aside to let the horses pass over the glittering moat. By then the sun was high, making Ellie sweat under her filthy clothes. She tried not to be impressed by the castle but kept tucking away details of it to tell Ralf about later—if there was a later with Ralf in it.

She saw slit-shaped windows in the watchtowers, designed to let arrows out and nothing in. The walls they passed through were as thick as Ellie was tall, and the baron's yard bustled like the village square on a holiday. She saw servants carrying stacks of cloth, chamber pots, a brace of plucked chickens. A girl with bare feet walked proudly at the head of a line of ducklings, who seemed to think she was their mother. Boys with dirty faces came to meet the horses and waited sullenly for the men to dismount. Even the baron's servants dressed better, and looked better fed, than the people in Ellie's village. Over all of it towered the castle's great keep, a dark shadow against the sun.

Ellie was dizzy with sleeplessness and shrank under the noise and curious eyes of the crowd. When ordered off her horse, she briefly considered running away. But she was certain she'd end up with an arrow in her back before she'd even left the yard.

A stout, sandy-haired man took the horses, and the rest of the men marched their prisoners over the green and into the baron's great hall. They spoke roughly among themselves as they went, while Ellie tried in vain to get close to the abbess. The men hadn't yet untied her hands, but she walked with her head held high, picking her way around horse dung and puddles. Maid Marian was bundled through the doorway first, disappearing into the dark.

The baron's hall smelled like dung and smoke and old meat, overlaid with the scent of fresh straw and dried lavender. It was nearly as noisy here as outside, as groups of servants moved among the high tables that ran along each side of the room, dogs snapping at their feet. It took a moment for Ellie's eyes to get used to the dim light; when they did, she realized that Marian had disappeared already. Ellie saw a man who was carrying a tray of chicken bones throw a meaty leg to one of the dogs, and she gasped. Half her village would give their last tooth to eat so well. Birds swooped among the beams of the ceiling, so high she could barely hear them chirping. At the head of the room was a high, carved chair like a king's throne—clearly the baron's. Though the morning was already hot, a fire burned in the hearth along the far wall, making Ellie even hotter. She still wore her tunic and leggings, though one was dark with dried blood and the other stiff with sweat. She sent up a prayer of thanks for the hidden hunting knife strapped to her leg, and wondered if it was a sin that she hoped for a chance to use it.

Two servants hurried forward to meet the baron where he stood at the mouth of the hall, one a broad, red-faced woman of middle age, the other a girl younger than Ellie, with sooty black hair hanging in braids beneath her cap.

"Prepare two rooms for my guests," the baron said. "And leave clothing for the girl. Bring me the tunic she's wearing, but burn the rest."

A small knot of noblemen standing as far from the fire as possible had watched them come in. Now one detached himself and swept toward the baron. He had a thin blond mustache and wore a rich purple cloak threaded through with glinting silver.

He greeted the baron in French so thick it took Ellie a moment to disentangle it. *Sister Mary Ursula would be right at home*, she thought bitterly. She'd always lorded her ability to speak French over the other nuns—but she wasn't the only daughter of a titled family to have taken refuge in the abbey. Sister Bethan spoke French as well as King Philip of France himself, and Ellie had learned much from her in four years.

Enough that she understood nearly every word the baron and his companion were saying. Each wished the other good health and a pleasant morning, though neither seemed to mean it. The purple-cloaked man's accent was unlike any of the sisters'; it came from his nose and buried half his syllables. Ellie stood still and made her face bland. Because she came from a peasant village, she knew they'd never guess she could understand the conversation. The hunting knife was sticky against her skin. *Let them misjudge me again*, she thought.

"Your hospitality does me a great honor," Purple Cloak was saying, "but I do not favor your damp country. I must return to France before it is the death of me."

*Return* to France? Ellie's breath came quicker. Was this man French-born, then? *But England and France are at war*, she thought with confusion. And everyone knew that the baron called himself King John's greatest supporter; he said as much whenever he demanded more taxes. "Your copper and grain will pay for the English army," she remembered him telling the villagers. "You want King John to defeat the French, don't you?" So why was he hosting a French nobleman at his castle? Was he supporting King John of England in public, and King Philip of France in secret? With effort Ellie stayed calm, while her mind raced. She didn't love King John, who was known to every peasant in her village as a greedy coward, and an enemy to Robin Hood besides. But if the baron could betray his own country, what else was he capable of? *Murdering Robin Hood*, she thought grimly.

The rest of the men's chatter was nothing but flattering pleasantries, until the baron turned and looked narrowly at Ellie.

"I must introduce you to my honored guest," he said, switching to English. "This is Elinor Dray, a novice at Kirklees Abbey."

He waited a beat, but Elinor neither curtsied nor acknowledged his words. She braced herself for a punishment, but it didn't come—though she felt sure that one could still be exacted later.

"She's quite the young heroine, in fact," the baron continued, a hiss in his voice.

"Oh?" Purple Cloak managed to inject the word with doubt, boredom, and politeness in equal measure.

"Indeed. She's the brave archer who finally slew the treacherous outlaw Robin Hood!"

Now Purple Cloak looked her over more closely, while directing his words to the baron. "Do you really think people will believe this nun—this *child*—killed the infamous Robin Hood? Even in France we have heard the legends. Surely the man was a better fighter than that." He spoke in French, but his words jolted Ellie to her core: He knew the baron was lying, and he didn't care. He talked about her fate as if it were no more interesting than that of a chicken. She fought to keep her murderous thoughts from showing on her face.

"He was an old man," the baron said dismissively, also in French. "And these peasants are no better than animals. They'll listen to anyone who carries a sword, and they'd barter away their mothers for a haunch of venison or a pretty cloak." In a low voice he began a story that involved an innkeeper's daughter and a string of glass beads.

Ellie tried to ignore his words, staring at the smoke-smudged walls of his castle. A servant was edging toward them. He had thin, greasy hair pulled back into a tail, and walked in a manner so odd Ellie stared, until she realized that what she had mistaken for a hunch was simply an extended, obsequious crouch.

"What is it, Gilbert?" the baron asked.

"My lord," he said, his voice as oily as his hair. "I have prepared a guest room for the young lady." A ring of keys jangled at his belt. Ellie's fingers itched, imagining how she might snatch them from him.

But two guards flanked her again, and Ellie was led up a winding staircase, then down a narrow stone hallway hung with guttering candles. She nearly screamed when a rat rustled in the straw under her feet, and almost laughed with surprise when they startled a man relieving himself in a corner.

Finally Gilbert stopped in front of a carved door and opened it for her, his eyes averted respectfully.

She stepped in and her jaw dropped. After the ugly squalor of the baron's halls, the room was opulent beyond anything she'd ever imagined. The walls were hung with intricate tapestries, the bed a high, carved thing covered in deep scarlet bedding. Beside it stood a curving candelabrum that made her think of a hart's antlers. Colorful birds twittered in a gilded cage, their tiny faces turned toward the light coming through the windows.

All Ellie could think was how just one of these rich

things—a tapestry, the glittering cage—could be sold for enough to feed a village family for a year. The half-starved forms of Ralf's younger siblings paraded past her mind's eye, filling her with a useless rage.

As she stared, the door closed behind her with a quiet rattle. A moment later a key scraped in the lock. Too late, she turned and rushed to the door, rattling it uselessly.

There was no response—she was truly the baron's prisoner.

Time passed. Ellie watched the sun rise to its highest point, then start the slow march back down. She found a chamber pot under the bed, and a Latin Bible. She tied and retied her hidden knife. There was a dress left for her on the bed, in a bluebell-colored fabric so thick and heavy it made her sweat to look at it. *What would Robin Hood do?* she asked herself, as she always did, even though the thought made her want to weep. By now it was time for vespers at Kirklees. Was Mary Ursula standing in the abbess's place at the front of the chapel? Whom would Sister Joan scold in Ellie's absence? Who would help Sister Bethan with serving, remembering the way her back ached if she didn't have help carrying the tureens?

Helplessness surged under Ellie's skin, until she took out her knife. She used it to work at the shutters over the window, finally getting them to open—but the long drop to the ground was too great to risk. Distant trees waved from beyond the baron's walls.

The birds cheeped at her softly, her fellow prisoners. She was eyeing their dish of seeds hungrily when the door finally opened.

Ellie's knife was still clutched in her hand when she turned. The woman at the door, the red-faced one who'd prepared her room, was carrying a tray. Behind her the empty hallway beckoned. Ellie took a step forward, hand tightening around the knife. Quick as thought, the woman dropped the tray and crossed the room. With an expert dodge and twist she got the knife out of Ellie's hands before she could react, then laughed again at her expression.

"Don't take it so hard, love," she said. "I had three brothers, and I could lay any of 'em flat with one arm behind my back. I'll assume that was your only weapon? Good, then. This can be our secret. You're a guest of the baron, remember—not his prisoner."

The woman let herself out, locking the door behind her. Ellie blinked away angry tears at the loss of her only weapon, the walls pressing in on her even more than before. When her hunger became worse than her fury, she descended on the scattered tray.

A goblet with some wine still in it, a hunk of bread,

and a stew thick with meat, only half of it spilled. She wondered whether she should eat the food provided by her captor—the man she guessed had killed Robin Hood, and knew had imprisoned her mother abbess. Then her stomach rumbled noisily. *What would Robin Hood do?* He would eat the food and have strength to fight, and think with a clear head. She couldn't right any wrongs if she starved. Ellie ate the meal so fast it felt like a hot lump in her stomach.

A faint cry came through her window. It sounded at first like a bird, or a child calling from far away. Then it resolved into the sound of her name. She jumped to her feet, knife forgotten, and dashed to the window. Sticking her head out, she looked down, then up, before realizing the voice was coming from the next window.

"Mother . . . Reverend Mother?" she cried.

"You can call me Marian now, I think." The abbess's voice was like a light in a dark room. Ellie could just barely see her if she craned her neck—a wisp of gray-threaded dark hair freed from her habit, her white hands gripping the edge of the window.

"Are you all right? Have they hurt you?" Ellie struggled to keep her voice even.

"Don't worry about me, Elinor Dray." The fearfulness Ellie had seen in her earlier seemed to have hardened

**LEAGUE OF ARCHERS**

into a new certainty. "I was and still am a noblewoman—the baron won't dare harm me until my trial."

Ellie said nothing. The abbess must know any trial put on by the baron would be a sham.

But Marian misunderstood her silence. "I'm sorry for keeping my identity a secret—from you and from the sisters. Like so many women who come to Kirklees, I wanted a fresh start. I couldn't have that if anyone knew my history."

"Don't be sorry," Ellie said fiercely. "You're Maid Marian. You're a hero. And Sister Mary Ursula would've sent you to prison years ago if she'd known."

"Forgive her if you can, Ellie. She, too, has a past she left behind."

"How can I excuse what she's done to you?"

Marian sighed, a wistful sound nearly lost to the breeze. "She was young once too. Raised in luxury by a noble family, the Beaumonts. Theirs is a common tale—a profligate father, too many daughters. By the time Mary Ursula's older sisters were married off, there was nothing left for her dowry. Some of the sisters come by choice, like Sister Bethan and Sister Ethel. But Sister Mary Ursula was forced to take orders. She had different dreams for herself, and the loss of them made her unhappy and unkind."

As the abbess spoke, Ellie could almost pretend they were back at the abbey. Ellie had been so angry after her mother died, so full of grief. The abbess had always spoken to her like an equal, even when they argued. When Ellie had woken with nightmares of her mother on the gallows, her eyes on Ellie's just before the baron's executioner kicked the block out from under her feet, the abbess had heard Ellie's screams and sat with her until she fell back to sleep. Now she was even extending kindness to the person who had given her up to the baron.

Ellie's eyes filled with tears. "You're so *good*," she said bitterly. "You don't deserve this. Mother . . . Marian, you could die!"

For a time Marian was silent. Ellie could see her hands, twisting together in the air beyond the windowsill. "I've lived my life as I wanted to," she said finally. "I ran away to be with the man I loved, and I was happy. When he left me, I ran away again, from a marriage I couldn't bear. The abbey was a good place to run to—it gave me protection, independence. It was the only place I *could* be independent, as an unmarried woman. Now, perhaps, it's time for me to stop running."

Her voice broke on the last word, and it clawed at Ellie's heart.

"No, it's not," she said firmly. "I'll find a way to save

you. The baron's lies mean one good thing, at least—
the way he tells it, I'm a hero. So he can't keep me his
prisoner forever. And when I get out, I'll tell everyone
the truth."

"I believe you," said Marian. "You remind me of
Robin in so many ways—his spirit, his faith in himself.
And his shooting arm, I think. When you get out, can
you do something for me?"

"Anything."

"Get word to the Merry Men." The words felt like
magic, coming from the mouth of Maid Marian herself.
Clinging to the window in her bloody tunic, hair in her
eyes, Ellie felt her heart begin to pound.

"If I am found guilty, I'll need their help." Marian
spoke faster. "There's a tavern called the Swan, on the
road to Nottingham. It's no place for a girl, or a nun, so
be inconspicuous—but start your search for them there."

Ellie was nodding, even though Maid Marian couldn't
see her. "I promise."

"Then promise me one last thing: If ever you feel
you're in danger when trying to help me, you must run."
Her voice lightened, and her next words reminded Ellie
sharply of something Robin had said. "I'll come out of
this all right—I've certainly come out of worse.

"And one more thing, Elinor Dray. Robin Hood is

gone from this world, but the world won't forget him. I know this because there will always be brave souls like you to continue his work. Just because he's dead doesn't mean our hope has died with him. Keep it alive, and never lose your desire to help others."

Ellie nodded again, her eyes stinging. "I promise," she whispered.

Somewhere in the castle the baron was weaving his plots, trying to ensnare both her and the abbess. But she was a hunter, a tracker—and a member of the League of Archers. She swore to herself she wouldn't go easy. She'd watch, and wait, and find a way to escape. And she would reunite Maid Marian with her Merry Men.

# 8

THE BED FELT THE WAY ELLIE IMAGINED A cloud might, soft and squishy and vast. When the sun had disappeared completely, she stripped down to her underclothes and settled in for what she expected would be a fitful night's sleep.

Instead she slept like the dead. When she woke up, the impassive face of the young, black-haired servant was hovering over hers. Ellie yelped and scrambled to her feet, forgetting for a moment where she was.

"There's clean water for washing, and a dress to put on when you're through," the servant said. She pointed at the blue dress, which she'd moved from the floor to a stiff-backed chair so covered with gilt Ellie hadn't dared sit on it. Snowy clean underclothes lay on top of the pile. The girl curtsied shallowly, then hesitated, looking at Ellie's face.

"Did you really do it?" she asked. "Did you really kill Robin Hood?" Her voice was a mix of awe and disgust.

Ellie shook her head desperately. "No, I . . . ," she began, but the girl was already backing away.

"The baron can call you a hero till kingdom come," she said, her words tumbling over one another to get out. "But you ought to be ashamed of what you did." Her courage gone, the girl fled from the room, slamming the door behind her.

Her furious face hung in Ellie's mind as she washed, dressed, and ate the bread and water left for her. Would it really be this simple for the baron to convince people of her guilt? Surely the people in her own village wouldn't be so easily led—half of them had known her since before she could walk.

Her unease only grew when the oily-haired servant came back with a guard to fetch her and escort her down into the crowded courtyard. The baron's men, stone-faced soldiers and comfortable-looking nobles, mingled with stiff-backed Frenchmen in their purple cloaks and servants moving in every direction to do the baron's bidding. Ellie had never seen so much finery in one place. She winced against the glare and the foreign feeling of the sun hot on her hair. Though she never hunted in her habit and headdress, she hadn't been out in full sunlight without them in four years. In the crush of people and horses she felt naked.

In the center of the courtyard was a cart, where two armed men and a driver waited. Ellie planted her feet in the dirt, not wanting to go anywhere near it. "Where are you taking me?" she said to the oily servant, who was treating her with far less civility than the night before. He smirked at the quiver in her voice and gave no answer.

When the baron finally appeared, his fresh-shaved face glowing with good health and his smile as crafty as a cat's, the Frenchman with the blond mustache was beside him. Under their gaze a guard heaved Ellie up into the waiting cart, pushing her onto a plank seat that ran across the cart between the driver and the guards. Then he tied her feet together with rope so she couldn't run away. She sat rigid, her face burning, as a laugh ran through the gathered crowd.

Then it fell silent, heads turning toward two men carrying something heavy between them. When they got closer, Ellie could see what they were carrying. Not what—*who.*

Robin Hood. Robin, her hero, his face slack. His

bared shoulder a purple bulge, filled with the poison she was certain could be traced back to the baron.

*No, no, no,* Ellie thought as the men carried the body closer, then threw it down beside her. One of his arms flopped awkwardly over the shallow lip of the cart, and she wanted, foolishly, to straighten it. She looked away, eyes prickling, as the smell of rot reached her nose. She thanked God the abbess wasn't here to witness this cruelty.

The baron swung himself onto his black horse, then wheeled around to face the people. "The great Robin Hood!" he called, gesturing toward the body with a flourish. "And the girl who heroically ended his life, young Elinor Dray!"

A halfhearted cheer rose from the crowd. For every nobleman's face that laughed and smiled, there was the angry face of a servant, watching her mistrustfully. *Can't you see he's lying?* she wanted to scream.

Instead she turned toward the baron, who rode beside her as the cart left his yard. "As your *guest*," she said through gritted teeth, "I demand to know what you're planning to do with me."

"I trust you had a pleasant night's rest?" he replied blandly. When he got close enough, her nose wrinkled at the sickly herbal scent drifting off what was left of his crow-black hair. It smelled like the tinctures villagers used to prevent baldness. "As for what I'm going to do with you, I wouldn't want to spoil the surprise."

Ellie felt sicker the closer they came to the village. What would they think of her in this ridiculous dress? What would they make of the baron's lies? The road into the valley was steep, and her stomach dropped as the cart clattered carelessly downward, penned in on either side by men on their horses, so close any of them could lean out and grab her if she tried anything. Too soon the village bobbed into view. When they passed the first houses, a few curious figures gathered in windows and doorways. Ellie spotted Margery's eldest sister at the side of the road, her pregnant belly straining the coarse weave of her dress. She raised a hand at Ellie, then dropped it, unsure.

Two guards sat behind her in the cart. As they approached the town's center, the guards stood and lifted Robin's body, draping it over the side. Then they straightened, and beat their shields.

"Hear ye," one of them cried, his voice booming through the morning air. "The notorious Robin Hood has been killed! The outlaw Robin Hood is dead!"

Now people streamed steadily into the muddy byways of the village, their faces touched with curiosity and dread. Ellie thought she saw Alice for a moment in the crowd and tried to catch her eye.

But nobody had eyes for anything but Robin Hood. Ellie saw the moment the truth of the guard's words hit their faces. A wave of grief and anger rippled through the crowd. Then William Mason charged forward, flanked by his broad sons. "Who was the murderer?" he cried in a voice that sent fear down Ellie's back. After that the crowd started yelling back at the guards, pressing against the sides of the cart and the flanks of the baron's horse. Ellie sought a friendly face, but already they were looking at her with suspicion, just for being in the baron's company. William and his son Thomas grabbed at Robin's body, trying to save it from the baron's blasphemous treatment, but were pushed back with the flats of the guards' swords.

By the time they reached the square, it seemed the whole village had gathered to watch them. Seeing their faces fall as they spied Robin's body was like watching him die a second time. Lucy Mason cried into her hands, and Catherine Baker into her floury apron. Children too young to understand clung wide-eyed to their parents. As men gathered in mutinous clusters, Ellie prayed they wouldn't try anything foolish—she doubted they were a match for the baron's soldiers. Jacob stood between his parents near the back of the crowd, and Ellie tried to meet his gaze. She told herself it was the glare of the rising sun behind her that kept him from looking back.

Then the baron dismounted from his horse and climbed into the cart. He grinned, as if he fed on the crowd's fear and rage.

"It's true," he cried. "The great Robin Hood is dead! The hero of the people, the keeper of your flame of hope."

*He's enjoying this*, Ellie thought furiously.

The baron smiled again. "The outlaw who defied the Sheriff of Nottingham himself was killed last night—at the hand of this girl." He reached his arm behind as if welcoming a noblewoman. "I give you the murderer of Robin Hood: Elinor Dray."

A thick silence followed this pronouncement, then a figure surged out from between two men.

It was Ralf. Ellie's heart jumped at the sight of her best friend standing brave and alone, his chest heaving with anger. "That's impossible!" he cried. "She would never!"

At a signal from the baron the man in the purple cloak rode toward Ralf, using his horse to cut the boy off from the cart. Ellie gasped as the man's arm rose, then fell. She heard the sharp hiss of a whip and Ralf's brief cry.

"She is the killer," the baron continued. "The girl is, for a nun, a very talented archer. We must thank her for ridding us of a dangerous villain." His face grew sly, and he drew something from his saddlebag, a wrinkled and wretched piece of cloth.

"No," Ellie whispered, her vision starting to swim. It was the bloodstained tunic she'd peeled off the night before. She should have hidden it or thrown it out the window.

The baron held it up so everybody could see its size and the gouts of dried red. "These are the clothes she wore! Some would have burned the garment, but I know how misguided many of you are on the subject of Robin Hood. So I'm gifting it to you. Perhaps you can bury it in your graveyard, in honor of the deceased." He smirked and dipped his head in mocking respect.

Angry murmurs began to spread through the crowd. The tunic felt like proof to them, when they wanted someone to blame. And everyone knew Ellie could shoot—many of them had eaten her poached meat. Now the faces watching her grew suspicious and cold.

The baron reached into his cloak and withdrew a velvet sack. He extended it slowly toward Ellie, who squeezed her hands together in her lap.

"It gives me great joy to do this," the baron said triumphantly. "In keeping with the law, I present the slayer of Robin Hood with this purse of gold. Elinor

Dray, by command of the king and as a reward for the killing of Robin Hood, this gold is yours."

Ellie felt the tip of a guard's knife pressed into her back, at too close a range for anyone in the crowd to see. "Now stand up and accept your prize, girl," the baron hissed. "Rise!"

Ellie surged to her feet. "He's lying!" she screamed—and the guard's knife pierced the heavy blue dress, drawing a gasp from her as it cut into her skin. She felt a trickle of blood mingling with sweat in the small of her back.

The baron pressed Robin's bow into her hands. Despite her horror she felt the rightness of its weight and clung to it like a drowning man clings to a thrown rope. Then the baron held up the red-fletched arrow. "It was with this poisoned arrow that she did it," he said. "A clever trick—the wound was slight, but he couldn't hope to fight against the poison's taint."

When Ellie opened her mouth to speak, the guard pricked her back again. She moaned instead, swaying on her feet.

"By the king's decree," the baron said, "you must applaud this girl. She has delivered a fugitive at last to justice. Now applaud."

All around the cart hands went behind backs and

arms crossed over chests. Not a single person clapped. Ellie's pride in the villagers mingled with her horror that they believed she could do this thing. She spied Margery in the crowd, her soft face open and shocked. Shocked at the baron's nerve . . . or at Ellie's betrayal?

Now the second guard and the driver jumped from the cart, their boots tramping hard into the dirt. They moved among the crowd with their swords out, saying things Ellie couldn't hear. It wasn't until one of them grabbed little Jonah Ward roughly by the shoulder and held a sword to his throat that the villagers started to clap.

The applause moved through the crowd like a poison. Ellie stood frozen, watching their faces turned toward her in shock and hate. Each clap felt like a tiny blow.

Then the baron signaled for them to stop, and the clapping guttered out like a candle. "The actions of Elinor Dray had other consequences," he said. "She exposed corruption at the heart of Kirklees Abbey itself. Within a house of God another outlaw found sanctuary: Maid Marian has been hiding there, in the guise of an abbess. For her crimes I had no choice but to have her arrested. In keeping with the law and with my own code of honor, she will stand trial for outlawry in a few days' time."

This second strike was too much for the village. All

around the cart angry rumbling broke out and tears began anew.

The first clump of mud took Ellie by surprise, thwacking against her shoulder like a rock. She was still looking for the one who threw it when a second hit her in the stomach. She doubled over as it knocked the wind out of her.

"Traitor!" Catherine Baker cried, her red face twisted. "Murderer!"

Her voice signaled the breaking of the dam. Suddenly the air was thick with pelted things—rocks and horse dung and clods of mud. A ladle flew by Ellie's ear as she ducked, unable to move too far because of her roped feet.

The crowd had shifted and she could no longer see her friends, but old Edmund Cole got close enough to speak. He was once the Drays' nearest neighbor, and seeing him always made Ellie think of the peaceful life she had known when both her parents were alive.

Now Cole looked at her like she was lower than dirt. "Your mother and father would be ashamed of you," he said, his voice ugly. "They're better off dead than seeing a child of theirs come to this!"

Ellie's heart felt like a broken egg, hurt seeping into her stomach and making it burn. He'd known Ellie since before she could walk. All of them did. They'd laughed with her parents, watched her grow up. How could even one of them believe she was capable of such a horrible crime?

When she caught sight of Ralf again, he was clinging to Alice and Margery, and there was a bruise over his cheek from Purple Cloak's whip. In their faces she saw blank shock, no sign of whether they'd been convinced of her guilt.

The villagers' cries were turning bloodthirsty. They'd gathered around the cart and started rocking it. Ellie fell back hard onto the bench, her feet straining against their bonds. The baron's horse tossed its head mulishly as he pulled it backward through the crowd, looking fearful for once. Then one of the lumps of dung meant for her sailed over her head and hit the guard behind her square in the face. As he reeled backward, swearing in disgust, his knife hand windmilled past Ellie.

In a flash she grabbed his wrist. She yanked the blade from his hand, then wheeled around and struck him with Robin's bow, still clutched in her other fist. He fell sideways off the cart and into the teeming crowd.

Ellie had no time to be horrified by the way they seized on him with fists and battered him with rocks. She hunched forward and sawed at the ropes binding her feet. The baron saw what she was doing and screamed at his remaining guard, but the cart was surrounded by angry peasants. *The constable got his revolt*, she thought wildly.

When her feet were free, Ellie looked down at familiar faces, twisted with anger and grief. Then, pausing only to grab the purse of coins, she jumped between their reaching arms, falling heavily into the dirt.

She half crouched, half ran, through the crowd. Andrew Newgate, who used to play horseshoes with her father, grabbed her by the hair; she felt strands rip away as she struggled from his grip. Yellow-haired Lucy Mason, who Ellie used to think looked just like a princess, drew her head back and spat. She shrieked as Ellie thrust out her knife.

"Get back," Ellie gasped. "Get back!"

"She murdered a man yesterday," Catherine Baker cried. "She'll do it again!"

As Ellie slashed out with her knife at anyone who got too close, they started to fall back, murmuring— remembering she stood accused of killing the greatest outlaw in Nottingham. Before they could regain their courage, and cursing the heavy skirts of her dress, Ellie fled for the gap between houses.

# 9

JUST GET TO THE WOODS, ELLIE TOLD HERSELF,
ignoring the pain in her back and the dress that tangled
her legs at every step. She ran full out and, when the trees
were close, dared a glance over her shoulder.

There was a crowd of villagers hot on her heels—old
Helen Pygott wielding a bucket, one of the bigger Ward
boys with a slingshot, a crowd of others she'd known all
her life, flushed red with rage and exertion. As Ellie
broke into the tree line, Catherine Baker crashed heavily
after her, grabbing at her skirts.

"Look at you—in your fine things!" she panted.
"You're in the baron's pocket, you murderer!"

Ellie swung the bow. "Please! Listen to my—"

Catherine threw a fist at Ellie and missed; while she was still off balance, Ellie darted away.

*Nobody knows these woods like me*, she thought grimly. As she ran, dodging grasping hands, ducking under fallen trees, and sliding through hidden drops in the undergrowth, the thought ran through her mind like a prayer.

*Nobody knows these woods like me.* She crossed a stream in three hops, hearing one of her pursuers crashing into the water behind her. *Nobody knows these woods like me.* She slid on her belly under blackberry brambles, hoping no one was small, quick, or crazy enough to follow her.

Ellie ran like a wild thing, until every inch of her was covered with sweat or blood or long white scrapes beading with red, from branches and thorns and all the other unfriendly parts of the forest. When she finally stopped, the sun was low, her heart felt like an animal in its death throes, and she ached in places she didn't know it was possible to ache.

Wearily she hauled herself into the branches of an oak tree. She clung to its trunk, listening for the sound of anyone giving chase. She heard far-off shouts, but soon they gave way to crickets and the lonely rustle of the forest.

Ellie shifted into a more comfortable position against the tree's trunk and considered her situation. Her skirt was torn nearly to ribbons, but her underclothes seemed largely intact. She still held Robin's bow, so tightly it had made a ridge in her palm, and miraculously the knife she'd stolen was still in the sleeve where she'd stashed it. The purse of gold was stuffed into her bodice. She didn't want anything of the baron's touching her, but . . . *What would Robin Hood do?* He would use the coins to fight the wrong and help the good.

She climbed down from the tree and followed the noise of water to a rustling stream. There she undressed, laying the abused dress over a tree branch and peeling her underclothes carefully away from her scraped-up skin. She washed the clothes and herself as best she could and gulped down handfuls of water until her empty stomach churned.

When she was clean, and her clothing passably dry, she slid back into the borrowed finery and used a piece of fabric from the skirt to tie her knife to her leg. Then she sat down on the stream's bank, finally letting her quivering muscles rest.

As soon as she stopped moving, the full weight of isolation crashed down on her. She was alone in the woods. She couldn't return to the abbey—Mother Mary Ursula would send for the baron faster than she could blink. The village had turned against her. She could never return there again.

And the League of Archers . . . had they turned on her too?

She had to stop turning everything over and be practical—she had to stay alive. She'd never spent a whole night in the forest before. Maybe the baron and the villagers had stopped looking for her because they knew the forest would do their work for them: Here in the trees, next to unarmed, she could be eaten by wolves. She could be set upon by outlaws—most of them weren't heroic like the Merry Men. And if she tried to return to her hiding place in the tree, she was likely to fall out of it the moment she fell asleep.

The meeting place. It was the only spot in the forest where the villagers might think to find her—but only if the League led them to it. The seed of hope that thought planted was almost painful. She shouldered Robin's bow and set off for the clearing.

It felt foolish to get this close to the abbey, but she couldn't think of a better plan. As she went, she gathered bits of dry wood, hoping that she could risk a small fire once she arrived. She was close to dropping with hunger and paused at a blackberry bush, filling her mouth with unsatisfying handfuls of tart fruit.

Ellie's heart quickened as she approached the meeting place. She pictured Ralf and Alice and Jacob and Margery waiting for her there. *They'll say they never believed the baron,* she told herself, *not for one second, and they'll have thought to bring bread with them.* . . . Her stomach gurgled and she ran the rest of the way.

The clearing was empty. She turned around once to make sure, then forced herself to kneel down and use the wood she'd gathered to start a fire. Her eyes filled, but she blinked the tears away. She cursed herself for spending too little time on the survival parts of outlaw life, beyond how to feed herself with berries and game. The woods were dark now, and the fire little protection against the night air.

It had all started with Robin Hood. She remembered every word of their meeting in the woods and regretted all the things she didn't say, not knowing who he was at the time. What if she'd gotten the arrow out right away— what if she'd thought to clean out the wound? For once she couldn't bear to ask herself what Robin Hood would do. Instead she clutched his bow in her arms and wished he were sitting beside her, to *tell* her what to do.

She was so miserable she didn't hear the sound of approaching footsteps until it was too late. She leaped to her feet just as a figure stepped into the clearing, her limbs surging with the impulse to fight or to run.

It was Ralf. He stood at the edge of the trees, gaping at

Ellie with her wild hair and torn dress, the knife in one hand and the bow in the other. A thin red stripe ran in a crooked line from his temple to his lip—the mark of the Frenchman's whip.

"I didn't do it," she said. "He's lying, Ralf, you know he is."

He moved closer, and she tightened her hand on the knife. He glanced down at it and grinned, but it was a sad ghost of his usual smile.

"You don't really think I'd believe the word of Lord de Lays over the word of Elinor Dray, do you?" he said firmly. "I know he's a liar, and so does half the village."

Ellie's shoulders sagged, relief as pure and bracing as river water flooding her limbs. She dropped her weapons and ran to Ralf, hugging him.

"That doesn't mean you can come back," he said when they'd broken apart. His eyes were as serious as she'd ever seen them. "The ones who do believe the baron are louder than the ones who don't, and they're whipping up anyone they can into a mob."

"Tom Turner?" Ellie asked sourly, naming the village's nastiest resident. Now he made his pennies selling his foul home-brewed liquor to the villagers, but as a young man he'd been a debt collector. He'd never gotten over his love of delivering bad news, and when he wasn't drinking, he was slinging complaints against his neighbors. His own wife had fled with their child years ago to escape his fists and bitter tongue.

Ralf nodded shortly. "Him and a few others. It's almost like they want it to be true. Just so they have an excuse to get angry."

Ellie flopped down next to her fire, feeling more sadness than rage. The baron had said the villagers were fools, ready to believe whatever lie he fed them. How disappointing that he should be right.

"The mother abbess asked me to find the Merry Men if I managed to escape—Maid Marian, I mean." Ralf's eyes widened at the words. "And she also made me promise to stay out of danger. But, Ralf, I'm *sure* the baron is the one who killed Robin. I don't mean the arrow came from his hand, but he must've been the one who gave the order. I can't keep both my promises to Marian—so what do I do?"

"We save Maid Marian," Ralf said, his voice utterly certain. "And when we've done that, we'll avenge Robin Hood too."

Ellie was too tired, too sad, and too hungry to think straight. She remembered the old man in the mob and his cruel words about her parents: "They're better off dead than seeing a child of theirs come to this." But she knew her mother would want her to do whatever it took to save Marian, the women who'd given Ellie a home when she no longer could.

Ralf crouched down beside her and began pulling things from the sack he carried over one shoulder—an egg, an apple, an extra cloak. "It's all I could grab," he said apologetically. "My father knew I'd try to meet you, so he wouldn't let me out. I had to sneak away." He pointed to the bruise on his cheek. "He doesn't want the baron's men to see me again. But don't worry—he believes you didn't do it."

The two of them huddled together in their cloaks. Ellie did her best to cook the egg, burning her fingers and sucking it down while it was still watery. With Ralf beside her and the stars overhead, the worst of the woods' horrors seemed to recede. As she slipped into sleep, Ralf taking first watch, her thoughts of rounding up the Merry Men and breaking Maid Marian free faded into hopeful dreams.

When she woke, the fire was out, a thin gray dew lay on her cloak, and Ralf had nodded off beside her.

And the person who'd woken her up still had his hand on her shoulder.

"Jacob!" she cried, sitting up.

"Some guard you are," he said to Ralf, who'd lifted his

head and was looking around blearily. "What if I'd been a pack of wolves?"

Ralf grumbled, and Ellie grinned. "I never believed the baron for a moment," Jacob said. "None of us did."

Behind him stood Margery, holding a basket of clothes, from which came the aroma of something that made Ellie's stomach growl. Beside her was Alice, who looked as put out as if she were the one who'd spent the night with twigs and stones digging into her back.

"The baron's a liar," Alice said, "and some of those idiots actually believe him!"

The last of the cold weight that perched on Ellie's chest rolled away. She was sore, hungry, and a fugitive on the run, but she felt suddenly happy. Her friends were beside her, and for a few moments that was all that mattered.

"I guessed that guard had a knife in your back," said Margery. "And I can tell by the way you're moving that I'm right."

Margery fed her, Ralf cleaned her wound, and Jacob kept them laughing every time someone threatened to get too sad. Alice stalked around the clearing telling them all the things she'd do to the baron when they captured him.

"We're not actually capturing the baron," Ralf said reasonably, after Alice finished a particularly colorful description involving a cesspit and a bees' nest.

"What do you mean we're not?"

"Ellie, tell her the plan," Ralf said. Now dressed in a fresh tunic and leggings, a sling of arrows over her shoulder, Ellie felt like herself again. The leader of the League of Archers.

She told them everything, starting with her late-night meeting with Robin Hood. She could see jealousy and sorrow warring in their faces, especially Ralf's. She told them about Maid Marian, and Sister Mary Ursula's betrayal, and her certainty that the baron was to blame— as well as her suspicion of his French guests.

Ralf touched his bruised cheek ruefully. "I don't have a high opinion of them myself."

With some pride she told them about the hidden knife and the shutters, and her conversation with Maid Marian.

"She told you to go to the Swan?" Jacob interrupted, sounding incredulous. "I've been there with my father, and it's . . . well, it's no place for ladies," he finished lamely.

Alice threw him a murderous look, and Margery rolled her eyes.

"Then it's a good thing none of us is wearing a dress," Ellie said coolly, twisting her hair up into the cap Ralf had loaned her, to make the point. "It's the only lead we have to go on, if we're going to find the Merry Men."

Everyone nodded in agreement, and Ellie tossed the baron's purse of gold onto the dirt between them. "And what about this, this . . . blood money? What should I do with it?"

"You should keep it," Alice said firmly. "You're a fugitive now. Whatever we do next, you'll probably need it in the end—to bribe someone, or to buy passage on a ship."

"We're going to clear Ellie's name and Marian's," Ralf said irritably. "Why would she run when she's done nothing wrong?"

Alice shook her head. "The baron will be looking for her. And the villagers will be more than happy to hand her over. More likely than not, she'll have to keep running for a while. Maybe forever."

"I think she's right," Margery said reluctantly. "The baron may be a rotten, lying coward, but he's powerful, too. His word is law."

Ellie looked at her friends' sorrowful faces and made herself speak bravely. "We'll save Marian first," she said. "And only when we're done will I flee."

# 10

IT WAS JUST AFTER DARK WHEN THE LEAGUE reached the Swan. They'd been making their way along the Nottingham road, deep enough in the trees that they couldn't be spied from any passing carts. Now they stood at the edge of the woods, staring at their quarry.

Their local tavern, the Beer and Bell, was a cozy place of broad beams and tucked-away windows, with ivy clambering over its walls. But the Swan was a blight, a one-story stone hovel that clung to the dirt like a crooked brown tooth.

"Well, there it is. The Swan." Jacob grinned at Ellie. "You want to run across and order us some ale?"

Alice hissed through her teeth, irritated, and Ellie shoved his shoulder. "We're not going in yet." She surveyed the grounds behind the tavern, covered in an array of even less reputable-looking outbuildings. "Follow me."

She took off at a run across the road, her friends at her heels. One by one they ducked into a reeking stable, close with horse smell and the sounds of whickering. Margery caught the first horse she saw gently by the nose and was best friends with him in moments.

"We need a plan," Ellie whispered.

"How about this: I sit on Ralf's shoulders, wrap a cloak around us, and go in there pretending to be King John himself," Jacob said with a straight face. "And I pardon all the Merry Men to bring them out of hiding."

"We need a *real* plan," Alice said. "Though I do like the idea of Ralf playing at being the king's backside."

"We could say we're apprentices," Margery said thoughtfully. "We can say our master is on his way to meet us."

"Apprentices of what?" asked Ellie. "Thievery? We need a reason to be asking after the Merry Men."

"And if anyone recognizes your face, you're done for," Alice said darkly.

Ellie looked around, as if the horses might have an idea—and suddenly she had one of her own. She grabbed a horse blanket hanging from a hook and draped it over her head and shoulders, propping the bow beneath her as if it were a walking stick.

Stumbling toward Ralf, she held out her hand. "Spare a coin for an old beggar woman, good son?" she rasped.

"Ugh," he said, flapping his hand in front of his nose. "Even if your acting isn't convincing, your smell will be."

She straightened up triumphantly. "The rest of you can be apprentices. I'll follow in after, and you can keep a watch on me while I see what I can learn. Nobody'll think to hold their tongue around a poor old woman."

They decided Ellie's gold would draw too much attention in a place like the Swan, but Jacob had a couple of pennies that would buy them a bowl of stew to share. They clasped hands for luck before heading into the inn.

Ellie made sure her bow and arrows were well concealed under the blanket. After a few more minutes she followed them.

The air in the yard was cool and pleasantly crisp, but crossing the threshold of the tavern was like walking into a solid wall of smoke and noise and warm bodies. The ceiling was low and the room was packed with long tables. A bar ran across the right-hand wall, and a blazing hearth along the left. She instantly felt foolish for thinking they'd stand out—none of the patrons took any notice of her, or of much else outside their own companions or cup of ale.

She watched a man slap a woman's hip as she delivered his tankard, and another one crash down drunkenly from his chair. She tried to imagine Mother Mary Ursula visiting the Swan, and bit down on her cheeks to keep from grinning.

She spotted her friends at a table against the wall, keeping a curious watch on the crowd. When Ralf caught her eye, she gave him a quick nod.

But finding the Merry Men wouldn't be so easy. They'd been with Robin when he delivered food to the village during the terrible winter, but how was she going to remember men she'd seen once, years ago, and only at a distance?

Ellie began sidling around the room, tapping her stick along the ground and hoping to pick something up from conversations. She paused too long at one man's elbow, and he turned around to glare at her.

"Have you any money for an old beggar?" she croaked nervously.

He turned away quickly and resumed his conversation. *Ah*, Ellie thought. *So that's the trick to remaining invisible.*

She managed to hear enough conversation at the next table—one man described, colorfully, a public hanging he'd been to in Shirebrook—to doubt the drinkers there would be of any use to her. When one of the men looked at her, she held out her palm.

"Money? Money for a poor old woman?"

He made a rude gesture, and she moved on.

The crowd at the next table was a rough-looking

       **LEAGUE OF ARCHERS**

bunch. But there was a woman among them, and it made Ellie think of Marian.

"Look elsewhere, old woman," one of the men said before Ellie could hold out her palm. "We've barely enough coin to feed ourselves, much less another hungry mouth."

Their table was covered with foaming tankards and the remains of a large dinner, and the sight made Ellie's tongue tart.

"Robin Hood would've spared a coin," she said. "He'd have helped an old woman out first, before buying himself more ale."

The man looked as if he was about to reply, but the woman at the table interrupted.

"She has you there, Geoffrey," she said. She pulled a coin from her skirts and cleaned it on her sleeve before placing it in Ellie's palm.

"In memory of Robin Hood, the greatest outlaw who ever lived," she said soberly. "And one of the greatest men."

Someone at the next table heard her words and stood, swaying, holding his cup aloft. Ellie could tell by his stance that it was the latest in a line of many.

"The death of Robin Hood was murder," he said loudly, "and I don't care who hears me say it!" Two of his friends rose to push him roughly back into his seat. Because you never knew, Ellie reflected, who might hear you in a tavern. She drew the stinking blanket closer around her as talk of Robin Hood spread through the room. If there was ever a time for one of the Merry Men to reveal himself, even accidentally, this was it.

"If I had me just a minute alone with the girl who killed him, she'd find herself shoveling coals beside the devil himself," said a man who couldn't have been more than twenty. "I hear she's on foot, so she can't have gone far."

Voices chimed in to agree with him. "They say she was one of us, too," an old man said. "A Midlands girl." He spat on the ground. "And her using a poisoned arrow . . . a coward's act. That's what it is."

Ellie ducked her head lower, more grateful than ever for her disguise.

Then an old soldier stood, his girth and his glower commanding the room's attention. "I don't wish to speak ill of the dead," he began.

"Stop talking before you do it, then," called a barmaid.

He scowled at her. "You all remember a hero, but I say good riddance. Not because he robbed from the rich, but because he killed too many good men."

His friend banged his cup on the bar in agreement.

"You'll find yourself in a ditch, talking that way in front of me!" the swaying drunkard cried.

"Not the way you hold your ale," countered the woman

who'd given Ellie the coin. "If it's a fight you're after, stay sober enough to win it."

"It's true," the soldier roared. "You only think of the wealthy, and Robin leaving them in pursuit of their own tails. You don't think of us who were sworn to protect the king and his people. You think Robin Hood stole their gold and then got away clean? No." He shook his grizzled head. "He fought his way out, one dead soldier at a time."

Shock made Ellie's stomach cold. She'd always been told that Robin Hood shot only to wound. But the soldier's words made her realize those were stories for a child. How could a man operate as an outlaw for twenty years without some killing? Just yesterday she'd fought her way out of her village with a bow and a knife. If she'd had arrows, wouldn't she have shot them if it meant freedom?

After the soldier spoke, the rumbling in the tavern took on a different tone.

"If you ask me," said the man who'd been talking about the hanging, "the Merry Men deserve what Robin got. They're troublemakers too."

"Robin Hood's thieving made no difference in *my* life," someone said. "He only made the sheriff come down on us harder—you could steal naught but a chicken, and he'd order your death. Said it would send a message to *all* the outlaws, but everyone knew which one he meant."

A woman stood, gripping her table's edge. "My son was one of those that lost his life for stealing—a bushel of apples. He was only fourteen, and soft in the head. I went to Robin and the Merry Men to ask them to save him, but Robin wouldn't even see me."

Now Ellie saw Ralf through the crowd. He was on his feet, fists clenched. Behind him Alice was tugging at his shirt. Ellie knew what he wanted to say, because she wanted to say it too: Blood on his hands or not, Robin *was* a hero. He'd saved their entire village. He'd saved their lives.

And now everyone thought she'd repaid him for that with a poisoned arrow, sent as a coward's gift in the dead of night—and worse yet, some of them thought he'd deserved it. She shook her head to clear it and caught sight of a broad-chested man with a cloth slung over his shoulder, a trio of mugs in one meaty hand.

"Excuse me," she said timidly. "Innkeep, sir?"

The man paused and cast a wary eye on her. "No food and drink but for those who can pay for it. We're not a church."

She took the measure of him—a man built like a bull, with a no-nonsense glare that reminded her of Sister Joan's—and decided to take a chance. "No, it's . . . the Merry Men. They sound quite dangerous. Do they ever drink at this tavern?"

**LEAGUE OF ARCHERS**

The man's face flushed and he seemed to grow an inch in size. "Not anymore, they don't. I've had to kick that rotten lot out for drunkenness and fighting more times than you have teeth in your head." He checked himself, peering down at her. "No offense to them who's too old to have teeth."

He looked around the room nervously.

"Just look at these men, half ready to kill one another at the mere mention of the Merry Men. They're nothing but rabble-rousers, and that's coming from a man who once called Robin Hood a savior."

Ellie backed away from the innkeeper, his words almost as unsettling as the old soldier's. As she turned, her eye fell on a man in a brown cloak who watched her from a corner table. His gaze was too steady; it unsettled her.

"Alms for a poor old woman," she muttered, making to move past him.

Before she could, he pulled a coin from his cloak and pressed it into her palm. "Here you are, grandmother," he said kindly. "May you find a soft place for your head and a warm place for your feet."

It sounded like a blessing he'd said before. Ellie looked at him more closely. He wore a rough brown robe, and his hair made a gray rim around his head, the scalp bare. He was a friar.

She narrowed her eyes, gazing back at him—then

a shouting match stole her attention. Two men were screaming in each other's faces, their friends standing angrily behind them. The argument about Robin Hood had risen in pitch and threatened to spill over into a brawl.

"I'd like to hear you say that in Robin Hood's presence," one of them growled, a wiry man at least forty years of age, with skin tanned dark as leather.

The man he spoke to was younger, no more than twenty, with an arrogant face and a crest of brown hair. "Your hero's dead, old man," he sneered. "And England's better for it."

Ellie dared a glance at her friends, catching Margery's eye. She was starting to jerk her chin toward the door, signaling them to follow her out and away from the brewing chaos, when the friar stood up and lumbered toward the brawl. She gaped up at him, as did those he moved past: He made the innkeeper look as slight as a girl. He was the broadest man she'd ever seen.

In the center of the room, the older man's hand had moved to his knife. The whole line of his body was taut, a wave ready to break. The friar clapped one friendly hand to his back and the other to his arm, saying something in his ear as he did so.

Amazingly, the man began to laugh—though it didn't reach his eyes. In another moment he shook the friar's hand, then returned to his table. The younger man sneered at his back, then returned to his own seat.

That was all it took. The perilous air of the tavern calmed as people turned back to their companions and the buzz of conversation began again.

Ellie's heart beat faster as the friar made his way back to his table. He was built like an ox and had a kind face creased with laugh lines. It wasn't uncommon to meet a friar, but to find one this big and strong, in a tavern known as a haunt of the Merry Men, could hardly be a coincidence. What if this was Robin Hood's right-hand man, Friar Tuck?

Once he'd sat down, she sidled over and plopped herself across from him, making sure to sigh heavily, the way Sister Bethan did whenever she laid down a load.

"It's a shame, their fighting over Robin Hood," she said craftily.

"It's always a shame, grandmother, when men turn to force without reason."

"Well." She tried again. "What might Robin Hood think of it? Some say he was a violent man himself— though others think him peaceable."

"Whether he's a saint or a sinner is not for us to say," the friar replied comfortably. "We must trust in God to sort it out."

Ellie sat back, chastened. If this friar didn't care one way or the other about Robin, perhaps she was eyeing the wrong man. But as he lifted his mug to his lips, he said something else that made her ears perk up.

"I think God will have no trouble with Robin, but he may have to work through Sunday to sort the Merry Men." He snorted at his own joke and took a slug of ale.

"But . . . do the Merry Men not work together?" she said quickly. "Don't their fortunes rise or fall as one— even in God's eyes?"

"You don't know of what you speak," he said kindly. "Their paths and Robin Hood's diverged long ago."

"Why? What happened?" Ellie said in her normal voice, popping up nearly straight before she remembered to hunch back down into her blanket.

The friar put down his cup and looked at her closely. Even in the dim torchlight Ellie wished for a better disguise. Then he reached out and grabbed her hand before she could snatch it away.

"Such young hands," he said, "for one so old. Do you care to tell me your secret?"

# 11

"I . . . YOU . . . YOU FLATTER ME, YOUNG MAN," Ellie said, putting so much creak into her voice it sounded false even to her own ears.

The friar smiled. "Hardly young, I would say."

"All men look young to one as old as I," she said hurriedly. "Thank you for the coin—now I must find another, before I seek a bed for the night."

Ellie hobbled toward her friends' table, feeling the friar's eyes on her back.

"Invite me to sit with you," she hissed at Jacob.

"Oh. Um, yes!" His voice carried over the crowd. "You must sit with us, old woman. You look . . . so very old."

She frowned at him and sat, her back to the curious

friar. "Now, *don't* all look at once," she said meaningfully, "but that friar who just broke up the fight is tall as a bear and seems to have some knowledge of Robin Hood."

Four heads swung to stare at him in unison.

"I said don't look!" Ellie said. "I think he saw through my disguise—"

"Because it's a horse blanket," Margery said reasonably. "A blind man could see through your disguise."

"So can a friar, apparently."

Ralf looked ready to explode. "Are you saying that might be Friar Tuck? *The* Friar Tuck? And we're sitting here talking about *horse blankets*?"

"If it is him," Alice said, "we'd better find out now. He's leaving."

Ellie jumped to her feet, fear of being discovered forgotten. "We have to follow him!"

Ralf stood up beside her, but Alice seemed to sink deeper into her seat, folding her arms over her chest. Jacob and Margery stayed perched on their bench, unsure.

"Well?" Ellie demanded. "What are you all waiting for?"

"Tuck was Robin's right-hand man," Alice said darkly. "If that *is* him, who's to say he'll believe you didn't kill Robin? We don't want to make another enemy. Especially one that's ten feet tall."

"Just look at this place," Ellie said impatiently. "Full

to the brim with drunks and fools. We can't go through them one by one, asking if they were ever in league with Robin Hood. If that man *is* Friar Tuck, he might be the only chance we'll ever get to save Maid Marian." She hunched back under her blanket. "Now, I'm following him. And I hope you'll come with me."

She moved through the crowd as quickly as her disguise allowed. Outside the door she sucked in great lungfuls of fresh night air, searching the yard for the friar. Moments later her friends tumbled out the door to meet her.

"One of those men tried to pull my cap off," Margery was saying grumpily. "I think he knew I wasn't a boy."

Then Ellie spotted him. "Look," she said. "He's getting away!" The friar was riding onto the road in an open cart pulled by two brown mares. As they watched, he headed in the direction they had come from—toward the village and the baron, away from Nottingham.

"We have to follow him," Ellie said, already pursuing the cart. "He can't be going far, unless he means to ride straight through the night—we'll keep behind him and check every inn we pass for sign of his cart."

"It won't be hard to stay *behind* him," Jacob huffed. They were moving as fast as they could through the scrubby trees by the side of the road. "He's got two horses, and we're on foot!"

"I can't be the only one who thinks this is a terrible idea," Alice grumbled.

Soon enough they lost sight of the cart completely. Then it rose again in the distance, where the road crested just before a crossroads.

"Keep up," Ellie said, panting. "We have to see which turn he takes."

"Wait." Ralf stopped completely, throwing his arm out to stop Alice. *"Look."*

They could see the crossroads in the distance now, lit by a flicker of orange flame. "There's someone there," Ellie said shortly. "The friar's cart has almost reached them."

They moved off the road and into the trees, just far enough that they could keep their eyes on the fire, which grew larger with every step. The shapes around it resolved into five men in too-familiar uniforms—the baron's men.

"Oh, God," Ralf said, his voice heavy. "Look what they've done."

There was something looming over the men, and now Ellie could see what it was: a gallows. On it hung the decaying body of Robin Hood.

Rage rose in her throat, tasting of bile. "His body should be buried, not on display," she spat. "He should've got what he wanted—to have a grave where his silver arrow fell."

They moved through the trees as quiet as deer, watching the friar's cart sway to a halt before the guards and their dreadful quarry.

The friar steadied his horses, then jumped down to speak to the men. Ellie saw with satisfaction that he was taller by a head than the tallest of the guards. As she watched, the men smiled at the friar's words, then laughed. One of them offered him a bottle, which he took.

"What is he doing?" she whispered. "I thought he was a friend of Robin—"

Before she could finish, the friar brought the bottle down on its owner's head. The League gasped as the man dropped like a sack of grain. In the surprised pause that followed, the friar kicked the legs of a second guard out from under him.

In the next moment the three guards still standing launched themselves at the friar, who, Ellie was now certain, could only be Friar Tuck. He'd pulled a dagger from somewhere, and even though he was old, he made the guards and their long swords look clumsy.

"It's him, isn't it?" Ralf's voice was wild in her ear. "Just look at him go!"

The friar was still fighting, but his movements grew steadily slower. He swerved out of the path of one guard's sword a beat too late, and it sliced across his shoulder. He looked down at the wound, just for a moment, and another guard made ready to stab him in the back.

That instant the world slowed down and shrank to the size of the friar and the man at his back. Almost without thought Ellie pulled an arrow from her quiver and strung it on her bow. It flew straight and true and hit the guard in the eye before he could bring down his knife. He fell down dead.

The friar looked straight at Ellie as the remaining guards yelled in surprise. A strange expression flashed over his face, before his attention turned back to the fight.

Now the battlefield calm that had fallen over Ellie was burning away. A hot panic took its place. She could see her friends gaping at her, their eyes ticking between her face and the bow in her hands.

The bow she'd just used to kill someone. Not a deer or an ox, but a man. She remembered the soldier's words in the pub, about Robin Hood's body count. And she understood that the friar had started this fight—the men were only fighting back, doing what they were paid for. Even if they were evil men, no amount of prayer could ever wash away what she'd done: committed a mortal sin.

All these thoughts flashed through her mind in one sickening moment. In the next, two of the guards were running toward them.

"May God forgive me," she gasped. Ralf looked at her with mute pity, then shoved her behind him.

She watched her friends take on the guards as if from behind a screen. The clang of metal on metal sounded distant to her ears. She kept seeing the man she'd killed fall to his knees. In her imagination his remaining eye turned to hers, and she watched it go dull as he died.

Then Alice's sword clattered to the ground beside her, and she snapped out of her shock. In one motion Ellie swooped to retrieve it, then tossed it back. Jacob held one guard at bay, his sword snapping like silver sparks in the patchy moonlight. He yelled as the guard went down, a wild, victorious sound that made Ellie feel cold.

Ralf had loosed an arrow into the man fighting the friar—but he had shot to wound. The man lay writhing at the friar's feet, the arrow in his side. Margery and Alice were circling the final guard. Margery's hair had fallen free of her cap, and the man seemed frozen between fear and irritation, that he should find himself fighting two girls. His expression settled on shock as Alice flung a knife that caught him between two ribs, then he fell.

The men lay on the ground, one moaning and the other

turning the air blue with curses. They were wounded but alive. *Only I took a man's life tonight*, Ellie thought. She shoved the thought aside and ran toward Friar Tuck, the rest of the League behind her.

The friar was watching them in frank astonishment. "You," he said, pointing at Ellie. "The old woman from the tavern, yes?"

She nodded mutely.

"There must be a story there, and I wish I were at leisure to hear it. But there's no time to waste. Help me cut Robin's body down."

In the end he was the only one tall enough for the job, but the League clambered around and helped him ease Robin Hood to the earth. Though the body stank like a privy and was barely recognizable, the friar held it gently in his arms and laid it reverently in the back of his cart.

Then he turned toward the League. "There aren't words enough to thank you for what you've done," he said urgently, "but you must run away home now, as quick as you can. I'll take care of Robin."

"You can't just bury him anywhere," Ellie burst out. "You have to find where the silver arrow fell—that's where his body belongs!" There were tears running down her face, and she worried her words sounded like raving.

The friar hesitated, the strange look passing over his face

**LEAGUE OF ARCHERS**

again. "I'll do right by him, I promise you," he finally said. Then he swung himself up onto his cart. "I must be off, as should you—seek a safe place and hide your weapons."

"But wait," Ellie said. "You can't go yet!"

The friar turned to her one more time, his patience cracking—then his gaze fell to the bow she carried at her side. His eyes widened and he seemed about to speak, but the sound of approaching horses stopped him.

"Run for your lives," he said grimly, flogging his horses into motion. "Until we meet again!" Then he was gone, and all of Ellie's protests died on her tongue. She hadn't even had time to tell him about Marian.

She swallowed down her frustration. "You heard him," she said. "Into the woods!"

The League moved away from the injured soldiers and those who approached on horseback, not stopping until the sounds of the road were overtaken by the nighttime hush of the forest. When they found a hidden space beneath the spreading branches of a pine, they ducked into it.

"We have to follow him again," Ellie said as soon as they'd stopped. "He went straight, and there's no other crossroads for a mile at least. We can go back to the original plan. I bet he'll lead us right to the rest of the Merry Men."

"No," Alice said firmly. "Maid Marian told you not to do anything that risked your life, and this is risking it." She spoke her next words to the ground. "And we have people waiting for us at home. People who couldn't get on without us if we got killed."

"Alice," Ralf reprimanded gently. But she just shook her head and pressed her lips together, looking as weary as Ellie felt. The fight seemed to have taken something from her—she might not have killed anyone, Ellie thought, but for the first time she'd turned her knife on a man.

Guilt filled Ellie's heart as she looked around at her friends. She couldn't keep asking them to endanger themselves. *What would Robin do?* If he was the person she thought he was—the person she'd believed in for as long as she could remember—then she knew the answer.

"I don't expect you to come with me," she said, "and I don't expect you to understand. But I can't give up on Marian. I just can't." She took a deep breath. "We'll always be the League of Archers. But I have to do this, even if I do it alone."

She looked at each of their faces in turn, reading fear and guilt and even anger there. Margery smiled sadly, and Jacob ran a hand through his dirty hair. Ralf shook his head slowly and opened his mouth to speak.

But Ellie thought of the little Attwoods waiting at home and spoke first. "I'll save her, and I'll clear my name," she swore. She tried to smile. "Then King John himself will have to offer an apology to me, and I'll decide whether I accept it."

Then she turned quickly and set her course for the road. She didn't look back.

# 12

BY THE TIME ELLIE REACHED THE EDGE OF the woods, the road was empty. However, a recent rain had left the dirt damp, and she could see fresh tracks from the friar's cart tangled with the stamping of the men on horseback who pursued him. The empty gallows cast a long shadow over the road.

Ellie smiled when she saw the place on the road where the friar's pursuers had given up the chase and turned back, not too far ahead. *Not worth the trouble when you've just had Alice's knife in your ribs*, she thought. She'd kept hold of the blanket, and now she pulled it back over her head, keeping one eye on the tracks as she moved toward the next crossroads. Her memories of traveling this road were mostly happy ones—sitting in the back of her father's cart when he had something to sell in a neighboring town, watching the trees for highwaymen.

Even then she'd dreamed of being a hero like Robin Hood—protecting her mother, going on a quest to bring her father home from the Crusades. Actually trying to be one was a lot lonelier and more exhausting than she'd expected. And dirtier.

The moon showed half its face, scraps of cloud chasing over it like dogs. Looking at it made Ellie feel even lonelier, so she turned her eyes back to the earth. By the time she was within sight of the next crossroads, she was wishing she'd taken time to eat something at the tavern. But all thoughts of a hot meal faded when she reached the turning.

It was a heavily trafficked road, and though the recent rain had smoothed some of the tracks away, dozens more remained. The marks of Friar Tuck's cart disappeared into a mess of ruts and hoofprints.

Ellie hunched in the middle of the road, hands on her knees, trying to read the tracks by moonlight. A wave of panic washed over her. If she couldn't find Tuck, what would she do next? She wasn't just a fugitive from the baron's crooked justice now, she was a true outlaw. A murderer.

She looked at her hands, small and parched and rough

with the work she'd done at the abbey. They'd held the bow that shot the arrow that ended a man's life.

*You can't take it back*, she told herself savagely. *It's done.* All she could do was continue down the path she'd started on, and hope the guard's death would be balanced out in the final reckoning. If she could save Maid Marian from the gallows, maybe he wouldn't have died in vain.

No matter how long Ellie stared at the cluttered tracks, the road kept its secrets. She stood straight, ready to scream with frustration. Her knees wobbled and she thought about picking a direction, any direction, and walking down it until she found Tuck or collapsed of hunger, whichever happened first.

Then she heard someone calling her name. She was too exhausted to feel anything but numb relief when the League trooped out of the trees, led by Alice.

"You ran off before we could talk it over," Ralf said. "But now we have. Robin Hood was an outlaw for twenty years with the help of the Merry Men. And when he finally died, he died without them. We can't do that to you."

Ellie nodded and stumbled forward to hug him. "As soon as we've found Tuck, you're going back to the village," she said into his shoulder. "Your families need you too."

She pulled back and gestured at the tracks, faintly illuminated by moonlight. "But it might be harder to follow him than I thought. Just look at this mess."

Alice hovered over the path, frowning. After a long minute she stood up straight. "That's him," she said, pointing down at the earth.

"How could you possibly know that, Liss?" Ralf protested.

She stared at him. "How could you not? Look, they're freshest, for one thing. And they look the same as the ones we saw before, in the tavern yard. And look here." She pointed at what looked like just one more indent in the road. "His horse favors his left foot."

The rest of the League stared at her a moment, dumbfounded.

"Well, that's sorted, then," Margery said finally. "I can't imagine anyone wants to argue the point?"

Nobody did, so they set off in pursuit of the tracks only Alice could identify. It was entering the deepest part of night, so they risked walking in the middle of the road. The stars peeked between ragged clouds, and the air smelled of rain and honeysuckle and the sweet green rot of midsummer.

They didn't speak much, not wanting to distract Alice from her study. After about an hour she stopped short, pointing toward the side of the road. "Look at that." She sounded perplexed. "The tracks go off the path here—straight into the bushes."

They all stared doubtfully at the thick layer of green. "Impossible," Ralf said. "Friar Tuck couldn't make it through there on foot, let alone in a cart. That could be anything—the tracks of an animal, maybe."

Ellie left the road and walked toward the thick hedge. When she pushed at it experimentally, it gave way. Excitement washed over her as she realized what Alice had led them to: a secret entrance into a seemingly impassable part of the forest. The bushes were cleverly cut into a living door that could be pushed back to make way for a cart.

The rest of the League gathered behind her, and she pushed open the hedge. They stepped into a dark green tunnel, barely lit by moonlight. For a moment the five of them just stood there, grinning at one another.

"This was always my favorite part of the Robin Hood tales," Jacob said. "Secret entrances into the forest! Messages hidden in trees! Traps laid for their enemies at every turn!"

"Traps that won't distinguish between enemies and friends," Margery said dryly. "Watch your step."

Alice took the lead, her eye for tracks and freshly broken branches leading them on a winding path so narrow Ellie could barely believe the friar and his cart had followed it.

"Look!" Ralf stopped and laid his hand on a tree trunk, where a pattern was carved into the soft wood. None of them could understand what it meant, but they were certain it was part of the Merry Men's secret language. The whole path spoke of their legendary presence. At times it seemed it was literally carved into the forest, with the ground cleared of undergrowth and branches cut away in great arcs overhead.

"Ooh, stop!" Alice called once, paused on her tiptoes before a thick fall of willow branches. "He took a turn here, sharp to the right."

On instinct Ellie moved beside Alice and pushed away the willow leaves that hid the path they'd been following, peering gingerly between them. Just feet from where they stood, the ground gave way to a deep ravine, so steep-walled and sudden it made her dizzy to look at it.

"There's your trap, Jacob," she said.

The woods at night *could* play tricks on you; she knew that from the League's hours of hunting by moonlight. And these woods seemed especially enchanted—half civilized by the Merry Men, half grown over and wild. Ellie almost expected to see forest spirits peeping at her from among the leaves.

Which was why she said nothing when she caught a glimpse of something. It was a here-then-gone flash of purple, as rich in color as the cloak of the baron's French friend.

*Could it be him, or one of the other French soldiers?* she wondered. Could he be following her—or Tuck? If so, why not announce himself, or pounce on her when she was alone? She stopped, then walked off the path, peering into the endless stretch of woods. Her friends' footsteps faded as she stood there, unsure.

Ellie walked deeper into the woods, knowing at every moment she should turn around. The trees rustled, and a far-off fox barked. A bank of violets had caught her eye, perhaps. Or nothing at all. She threw one last sideways glance through the trees, stepping forward as she did so.

As soon as her second foot left the ground, she knew something was wrong. The ground beneath her dipped with a sickening sag, making her stomach lurch. Ellie froze like a buck and stared down at her boots.

The hidden ravine wasn't the Merry Men's only trick. A net of brittle branches were all that stood between her and the mouth of an open trench. She was standing in the middle of a pit trap.

## 13

THE LEAGUE HAD DUG A PIT TRAP ONCE FOR rabbits, which a then six-year-old Alice insisted on baiting with clover flowers. When they went back to check it a day later, they'd caught a furious weasel. It was no rabbit, but hungry bellies couldn't complain.

If she'd been a man, the trap Ellie stood on now would've given way in an instant. She cursed herself: Even in the weak light she should've noticed the pile of brittle branches covered over with leaves, barely concealing the mouth of who knew how deep a pit.

She lifted one foot to step backward, but the branches creaked ominously as soon as she moved. Hastily Ellie dropped her foot back in place and gave a warning whistle, high and clear.

She waited, straining to see her friends coming toward her in the dark. But there was no answer, just the minute crackling of the branches below her. At any moment they'd give way and she'd be swallowed by the pit. She looked around to see if she could just *fall* back onto solid earth. No—she was too far from the pit's edge. But as she turned, she saw a thick coil of ivy trailing along the ground, just close enough to reach. Careful not to shift her weight, she crouched down and snagged it.

Ellie breathed out in a nervous rush when she was standing again. Carefully she removed an arrow from her quiver and tied the ivy to it, using an unbreakable knot her father had taught her before he went to war.

She strung the arrow on Robin's bow, feeling for a moment how the ivy threw off its balance. When she figured she knew how to make up for it, she let it loose. "*Yes,*" she hissed as it embedded low in the trunk of the nearest oak tree. Now the ivy hung in a loop just over her head. Bracing herself, she jumped up and grabbed it, pulling her legs to her chest, then propelling herself forward. The vine snapped, dropping her hard on the forest floor. When she peered down into the jagged hole they left behind, she saw nothing but a darkness so complete it made her shiver.

By the time she straggled back onto the hidden road, Ralf and the rest of them were there to meet her.

"Where'd you run off to?" Alice said, her relief cut with anger. "We thought a ghost had gotten you!"

"Or a baron," Ralf said darkly.

"Neither," Ellie said. "It was a pit trap."

She told them how she'd saved herself with Robin's bow. As they continued along the path, they saw another, badly concealed pit and worn-out snares made of frayed rope. Ralf got more excited at every sign of the Merry Men. Soon it wasn't just Alice who could see the path and all its markers—all of them felt they were getting closer to something, some secret place here in the dark.

Alice was still in front. She'd just disappeared through a space between two bushes when they heard her gasp.

Ellie rushed to join her, struggling through the grasping bushes. When she made it through, her mouth dropped in awe.

After winding for ages through the tight and secretive forest, they stood now on the edge of a vast clearing. The grass was silvery in the starlight, studded with some kind of night-blooming flower that turned the air sweet.

But what she stared at was the enormous oak tree in the heart of the clearing. Its trunk was gnarled and bulbous, its thick arms spreading nearly to the trees at the clearing's edge. The expanse of its branches seemed the size of a small village, and they bristled with strange shapes against the dark.

"It's the Greenwood Tree." Ralf's voice was filled with wonder. The Greenwood Tree was the stuff of legends. Everyone knew, without knowing where they'd heard it, that Robin and his men had made camp in the shade and branches of the greatest oak in Sherwood Forest, so deep and hidden that the Sheriff of Nottingham could never track them. Ellie never thought she'd actually see it.

She ran forward and looked up. Embedded in the tree's trunk was a series of steps, leading into the thicket of branches starting far over her head. The tree was hung with pulleys and studded with platforms, and here and there an enclosed structure like a tiny cottage, tucked up into the leaves. She put her foot on the first step and started to climb.

When she reached the first platform, she could see more clearly the ingenuity of the tree. Its branches held a sort of tiny village, with pulleys running between platforms to carry goods higher and higher, and hollow half logs lashed to strong outlying branches, ready to catch rainwater and be reeled back in. Ralf's grinning face appeared over the edge of the platform, and he hoisted himself up beside her. Laughing quietly in the dark, they climbed a worn rope ladder to the next level. It held a tiny wooden house that swayed slightly in place. Remnants of green paint stained a door barely taller than Ellie. She leaned close to the center of it, peering at the place where someone had carved letters deep into the wood: M+R. Her eyes widened, and she pressed her palm against the lettering.

She heard whispers and laughter as Alice, Jacob, and Margery joined them in the tree, ranging carefully through the Merry Men's home in the leaves. Even here they must not have felt completely safe—because just like the woods, it was booby-trapped. Margery grabbed on to a branch that bent forward like a lever, setting a winding stretch of rope to creaking and a branch set with sharpened spikes whistling down toward her. Ellie heard it shriek from over her head, and Margery cringed into a crouch. But the branch stopped before it hit her, caught against some chink in the mechanism. Ellie half slid, half climbed, to her friend, pulling the spiked branch free. Before she threw it to the ground, she saw something on its bark: a carving the size of her fist, flat on the bottom with three points on top. *A crown?*

Margery blew out a breath, hand to her heart. "I'm all right," she said. "The tree knows the difference between friend and foe."

Ellie laughed, but Margery shook her head. "I mean it.

Don't you feel it?" She flung her arms out. "They say this place is protected by the tree itself—or by the spirits that live in it. I could've been hurt just now, but I wasn't. The Sheriff of Nottingham could've found this place years ago, but he didn't. We're safe here, just like Robin and the Merry Men were."

But they moved more carefully through the branches after that, wary of other traps. When Ralf gasped, Ellie's heart jumped into her throat, but he was unhurt, standing on a platform just below her, staring at an old ringed practice target, shot full of arrows. He touched their fletched ends with careful fingers.

Ellie climbed all the way to the top, where a lonely watchman's platform swayed. She could see her friends in snatches through the leaves, and the tops of their heads filled her with tenderness. The ancient oak, too, gave her a feeling of comfort, as if it and the ground where it stood were hallowed somehow—free of the trickery and danger in the rest of Sherwood Forest.

Finally she climbed down, her boots the last to hit the ground. Before she could speak, Ralf grabbed her arm, a finger to his lips. Then he pointed toward the roots of the tree. They rose and tangled like plaits along the ground, and in a gap between two of them was a neat pile of charred sticks.

**LEAGUE OF ARCHERS**

"Firewood," breathed Ellie.

Hushed now, they crept around the base of the tree. In another hollow a dark cloak was spread out to dry. A low-hanging branch half hid a small, battered tent, and there were fresh horse tracks pressed into the ground.

Ellie glanced at her friends. Moving as quietly as they could, they followed the prints to a hazel thicket at the edge of the clearing. Behind it Ellie recognized the friar's cart, now empty. Beside it his horse pulled up mouthfuls of grass.

Then the sound of a bowstring being pulled taut made Ellie spin around.

Friar Tuck stood before the Greenwood Tree, an arrow trained on the League. He looked more massive than ever, his face like stone.

"Why have you followed me here?" he growled. Then, before they had a chance to answer, "And how? Nobody can find this place who isn't meant to."

Ellie could sense Alice planning to say something smart, so she hurried ahead of her. "I can explain. If you—if you lower your bow."

He stayed frozen in the moonlight, his arrow pointed toward her heart.

"You're Friar Tuck, aren't you? And I'm Elinor Dray." She saw his surprise as he recognized her name, and the way his hands tightened on the bow. "I had nothing to do with Robin Hood's death," she said quickly. "But I was there. I saw what happened."

The bow started to droop as she spoke, telling him about meeting Robin in the woods, her years at the abbey with Marian, the terrible riot in the village square. Everything up until the moment they tracked him all the way to this forbidden place in the woods. By the time she was done, his hands hung loose at his sides.

"You have to help us," she finished urgently. "For Marian's sake. Please."

He sighed heavily. "You'll need food and drink, at least. And rest, too." His voice was gruff, but he kept darting curious glances at them from under his stiff gray brows. "I still can't understand how you tracked me here, but I can say this—five years ago it was better protected. You'd never have gotten close without one of us knowing about it."

"But where are the rest of the Merry Men?" The words burst out of Ralf. He kept looking from side to side, as if he expected Little John and Will Scarlet and all of them to come spilling out of the forest at any moment, ready for a feast.

"Gone." Friar Tuck looked very old suddenly. "Drifted away, dead, in prison perhaps—God knows where, but gone. I hoped, after Robin's death, that they might—but no. I'm the only one still living in the greenwood."

"But why?" Jacob looked almost as sad as Ralf. He also looked so young next to the friar. Ellie could hardly believe he'd so recently wielded a sword against the baron's own guards.

"After what Robin did?" Friar Tuck shrugged. "I was foolish to think they would come back." He led them to his campfire on the far side of the Greenwood Tree's massive trunk, where something popped and sizzled on a spit hung over the flames. With a practiced gesture he reached up and yanked a length of rope hanging from a branch overhead. A moment later a small ale cask tumbled down into his arms. He smiled, just barely, at Ralf's gasp, then sat down heavily on a log beside the fire.

"What did he do?" Ellie asked, her voice small. She wasn't sure she wanted to hear the answer.

The friar just shook his head. "That foolish, selfish man," he said, almost to himself. "Now sit down, and have something to eat."

"How can you say that?" Ralf asked, his face angry in the firelight. "He was your leader—he was a hero, to everyone!"

"You're talking about the legend." The friar's voice was sharp. "But I knew the man." He sighed and softened a little. "He was as flawed as any of us. Worse, even. Perhaps the legend grew too large, until it suffocated him."

There was silence among the group as the words sank in. Ralf did not look ready to accept them.

"What have you done with his body?" Ellie asked. "I told you, you had to bury him where the silver arrow fell."

"I already have." He raised his brows at their looks of surprise. "I found the arrow in our other camp. It's closer to the edge of the woods, easier to find but good for a quick escape. None of the Merry Men were there, either, but Robin's arrow was, dug halfway into the dirt."

"But that's—that's magic." Margery had her church face on, wide eyed and awestruck. "How could he shoot from the abbey window and drop the arrow right where you'd find it?"

Tuck frowned a little as he stoked the fire. "I'm a religious man, so talk of magic doesn't sit right with me. But there's something about that arrow. There was never any question it would find its way to where Robin intended."

Ellie looked up into the branches of the Greenwood Tree, feeling a shiver go through her. Of course the arrow had flown where Robin sent it. He had a connection to the woods; she could feel it here, sitting under the arms of the great tree. She almost expected

Robin to climb down from its branches, a young Marian beside him.

"He's buried just where he'd choose to be," Tuck continued. "And I've said the rites. But I'm holding a funeral service there at midnight in two days' time—word is already being spread by a few people still loyal to our cause, wise enough to know who're friends and who're spies for the baron. All the men who once stood with Robin, and were saved by him a hundred times, will have one more day to get there, to pay their respects."

"Please, sir." Ralf finally sat. "We'd like to be there too."

The friar nodded. "I think you've proved you're true friends to Robin. And you'd probably find his resting place even if I didn't share it with you!" he said with a chuckle. He described the location of the camp, not far from the rocky place where they'd stood, shivering, the night they were chased by the gamekeeper.

"The last thing we need is the baron trying to take the body back," he said grimly, "which he'd do no matter how deep I buried it. So keep what I've told you to yourselves, and don't go trusting the wrong people."

He looked at Ellie kindly. "You especially should be there, in place of Maid Marian."

"But we have to *save* her . . . ," Ellie began, and the friar shook his head ruefully.

"It's only me now. An old man who needed the help of children to shake off a mere five men. Not that you are *ordinary* children, I'll give you that."

Alice looked as irritable as a nest of wasps, and Ellie felt no better. She was still a fugitive, her friends would leave her now that they'd found Friar Tuck, and she was no closer to helping Marian than when she was trapped in the baron's castle.

"So what do I do now?" she asked, her voice more plaintive than she meant it to be. "Do I forget Maid Marian and run, save my own skin? Robin Hood wouldn't have done that."

The friar looked at her sharply. "There you go again, giving the man a halo that never would have fit him. One thing Robin never lost was his sense—and as you're innocent, that means someone else must be guilty. Any ideas?"

"The baron," she said quickly. "I'm sure of it."

"Start with your village, then. If you can convince the villagers to believe you—to take you back in—perhaps you can live there quietly for a time, in hiding. Eventually the baron will find a new distraction. A new fugitive to chase down."

Ellie remembered the movement she saw at the edge of the woods, right after Robin dropped to his knees with a deadly arrow in his shoulder. Now she pictured the gamekeeper holding a bow as he melted back into the forest, or the Frenchman in his purple cloak, shooting Robin, then running like a coward.

"We have to go back," she said. "Back to where Robin died. What if we can find something there? A button . . . or a footprint, something left by the person who really killed Robin?"

Her friends' faces were skeptical, but she charged on.

"Can you imagine if we could convince the village that the baron is the one who killed Robin—then pinned it on a novice?" She grinned. "They'll revolt!"

"If we can tie up that loudmouthed Tom Turner and stick him in a haystack for a few hours," Jacob said slowly, "we might be able to change their minds."

"You could hide in our barn while we talk to them," Margery said. "If you don't mind sharing it with a new litter of piglets."

Even Alice warmed to the idea after a while, though she remained half-certain Ellie would be plucked up by the baron the moment she stepped clear of the woods.

"He can't be everywhere, Liss," Ralf said exasperatedly.

"Oh, can't he?" she replied. "He and his men are like mosquitoes in June."

Ellie wanted to set off right away, but she knew they

had been lucky to make it through the woods in dim light once. Tuck gave them good food: spitted rabbit and tiny charred potatoes, washed down with green-tasting river water. The meal took the shivery feeling out of her limbs and made a warm weight in her stomach. Tuck spread his cloak under the fading stars, giving his tent to the boys and a shelter of woven branches to Ellie, Margery, and Alice. "I'm too old now to be climbing," he said, gesturing at the wooden structures in the Greenwood Tree, "and I'd prefer you leave the tree to the ghosts tonight."

The shelter was barely larger than Tuck. It had a thatched roof and smelled thickly of smoke and green branches, and on the earth floor was a prickly, straw-stuffed mattress the girls flopped down onto. Alice's and Margery's breathing soon deepened as they slipped into sleep, but Ellie lay for a while. She could hear the Greenwood Tree's ancient branches creaking outside and the night air rustling its leaves. She felt safe for the first time since she'd been dragged from the nunnery. *Nothing can touch us here*, she thought. *Not even the baron.* Was that how Robin and Marian had felt about this place? Still wondering, she fell asleep.

She woke to the smoky, fatty smell of meat cooking. Friar Tuck fed them a breakfast of pork chops and bread, and filled their packs with enough food and water for the trip back through the forest.

"How you missed every trap I'll never understand," he said. "Just stay on the path and try to walk exactly the way you came. And don't get too close to any tree that has a certain carving on its trunk, looks like a—"

"A crown," Margery said. "Right?"

"*Any* carving," he said, watching her shrewdly. "Different symbols for different traps."

Before they left the clearing, he put one massive hand on Ellie's shoulder. "You carry his bow well," he said. "And you can shoot it too."

She nodded mutely, knowing Tuck was remembering the way she'd shot the guard down with one arrow through the eye.

"You should have this." He reached into his own quiver and pulled out Robin's silver arrow. Ellie drew in a breath.

"You know the story of how Robin won this arrow, yes? Well, it was never really meant to fly. It's a trophy, not a tool—until it came into Robin's hands. Some say it's magic, but I say it's blessed: It will never miss its target. But that means you must be very careful how you choose to use it."

He held the arrow a moment longer before giving it

to Ellie. She accepted it with both hands. The story he'd told sounded more like Jacob's myth than the adventure she'd told Gregory, the little boy in the hospital. She wasn't sure she could believe in a blessed object any more than a magical one. But she believed in the goodness of the man standing in front of her, and the humble magic of finding him first in a tavern, then in the center of a great wood.

The arrow was cool against her palms, heavy but not as heavy as she would have expected. She slipped it carefully into her quiver, welcoming the new weight of it on her shoulder.

# 14

BY THE TIME THE LEAGUE STUMBLED, TIRED, dirty, and scratched, back onto the Nottingham road, the worst of the day's heat had broken. It was harder getting out of the forest than it was getting in, maybe because they were less excited about where they were going.

They were walking in the sparse trees near the roadside when they heard a heavy cart approaching. Every time this happened, they'd melt a little deeper into the trees, watching to make sure the cart wasn't carrying guards or, worse, the baron himself. This time when Ellie peeked between trunks, she saw a cart laden with sacks, probably on its way to the Nottingham market.

But as the cart drew closer, she saw its driver more

clearly, and her heart turned over. It was Gilbert, the baron's greasy servant who'd escorted her to her room. Who'd locked the door behind her using one of the many, many keys on his belt.

Ellie moved forward slowly, narrowing her eyes.

"Uh-oh," Ralf said low. "I've seen that look before. What are you planning, Ellie Dray?"

"That's the keeper of the keys!" Ellie hissed. She could hardly believe their luck. With that key ring she wouldn't need anyone's help rescuing Maid Marian—she could simply sneak into the castle and unlock her cell door.

She grabbed her bow. "We have to hold up that cart!"

"Ellie," Margery said warningly. "It's broad daylight!"

"And we'll never get such a chance again. Robin's just three days dead, we can't already forget about him. Please," she pleaded. "We all know what a trial means to the baron: a show you put on while you're tying the noose. We're Marian's only chance at staying alive. Just trust me, and follow my lead."

Before they could respond, she ran out and planted herself in the middle of the road. The cart slowed as it came nearer, but didn't stop. It held three men—Gilbert, a gray-bearded guard, and a bored-looking boy of about twelve. He perked up when he saw Ellie, an unexpected distraction.

"Get out of the way, boy!" the guard yelled. Ellie's

hair was still twisted up into her cap, and she wore Ralf's hunting clothes.

"Stop your cart," she called out, then strung an arrow on her bow, aiming it right at the man's chest. He pulled the horses up short, scowling.

"What's this, a prank?" he grumbled. "Go home to your mother and drink your milk."

Now they were stopped just in front of her—almost close enough for the guard to leap down and pull the bow from her hands. *If he tries it,* she told herself, *I'll have to shoot. But this time I'll shoot to wound.*

But he didn't. Instead the boy jumped to his feet, face bright with excitement. "That's not a boy," he said, pointing at Ellie. "That's the girl who killed Robin Hood!"

Now Gilbert stood up, his watery eyes going wide. The heavy key ring swung from his belt like a pendulum. As Ellie tried not to stare at it, she saw a flash of brown on the road behind them—Jacob running swiftly across.

Did he have something planned? She prayed he did. She, on the other hand, would have to improvise.

"The baron lied to you," she said. "I'm innocent! And what's more, I can prove it. I have the Merry Men with me, and they'd never back the murderer of Robin Hood." She looked showily to the left and right, where she knew her friends were hiding.

The boy's jaw dropped, but Gilbert started to laugh. "Oh, do you, now? The Merry Men are naught but a story nowadays. Next you'll be telling me the Lady of the Lake herself is on your side."

The gray-bearded guard started to climb down from the cart. His hand reached for the sword at his belt.

Ellie needed help. She let loose a whistle, hoping her friends would do something . . . and to her relief, four arrows flew from the trees. Each hit one of the sacks the cart carried, splitting them open. The steady hiss of spilling grain was the only sound that punctured the shocked silence, until Gilbert started to yell.

"What are you waiting for?" he scolded the boy. "Stop up those sacks. At once!"

The boy ignored him, cowering at the bottom of the cart. But the guard had drawn his sword. His eyes ticked from Ellie to the trees. Quickly she dropped her arrow back into its quiver and retrieved the silver one. She strung it slowly and then aimed it right at the guard's face.

This arrow wasn't made for anything but a killing shot, and she knew she could never actually loose it. But the guard didn't know that. He stared at the arrow, then shook his head, blinking, as if he'd seen it wrong.

The boy, peeking over the edge of the cart, gasped as he recognized it too. "That's Robin's arrow," he said wonderingly. "It never misses its mark!"

The guard still held his sword aloft, but the anger on his face was cut with fear.

"The Merry Men will riddle you with arrows on my signal," Ellie said. "They'll spare nothing but the horses. But I *will* spare you if you do exactly as I say." Her heart trilled like a songbird, but she made her voice level and her face as hard as the baron's heart. "You'll all three step down from the cart and lie on your stomachs on the road, with your eyes to the dirt."

"How dare you!" squawked Gilbert.

But he climbed down from the cart, smoothing his oily tail of hair as he crouched to the ground. The guard scowled at Ellie, but he sheathed his sword and lay down too. The boy scrambled down beside them.

"Alan-a-Dale!" Ellie yelled. The boy gave a start of surprise as he heard the name of one of Robin's infamous followers. Alice emerged slowly from the trees, far enough behind the cart that the men lying on the road couldn't possibly see her.

Ellie fought back a grin. "Check the cart, Alan."

Alice grinned too. She jumped onto it and picked through the bags piled there, stuffing a few things into her sack. Ellie reached down to Gilbert's belt and unfastened the ring of keys.

"You can't take those!" he spluttered, starting to sit up. Ellie stood back just far enough to aim the silver arrow at him, and Gilbert fell silent and flopped back onto his belly.

Alice gave Ellie a nod, letting her know she was finished with the cart, then hopped down and vanished into the trees. Ellie pulled the boy to his feet. He was a little older than Alice, with freckles and brown hair that stuck up like feathers.

"Do you see that tree?" she said, pointing into the thick, leafy crown of an elm. She made sure her voice was loud enough that Gilbert and the guard would hear every word. "I've commanded Will Scarlet, the cleverest of my men, to wait in it and guard you." On the ground Gilbert gave a yelp. "If any of you so much as moves before the shadow of the tree has covered the road, he will shoot you!"

The boy nodded in numb terror. When she let go of his collar, he hurled himself to the ground and drew his arms over his head.

Ellie walked slowly into the trees, as if robbing the baron's men were something she did every day. But as soon as she was out of sight of the road, she broke into a run. A laugh exploded out of her, and she felt like she could run for hours. She'd never thought stealing from the rich would be so easy!

# 15

ELLIE AND HER FRIENDS RAN UNTIL THEY
reached their meeting place. She had never loved
being part of the League of Archers as much as she did
right then. She felt like they shared one head and one
heart, sprinting nimbly through the forest as if they'd
never stop.

In the clearing they bent over their knees, panting
and laughing. Even Alice's face looked carefree.

"You had them believing Robin himself was going to
walk from the trees," Jacob said. "They would've danced
a jig in nothing but their belts if you'd asked!"

"But why on earth would she want them to?" Margery
added, giving an exaggerated shudder.

Ralf jogged his sister's shoulder. "Let's see what you've got, Alice. You've stolen from the rich, now it's time to give to the poor."

Alice pulled a small coin purse from the front of her tunic and dumped its contents onto the grass. It was far less than what the baron had given Ellie, and none of it gold, yet it sparkled in the sun like pirate's booty.

"We'll divide it five ways," Alice said.

"Four ways," Ellie said, patting the gold hanging from her belt. "Or better yet, do it in five, and give my share to the village."

Margery's eyes lit up. "Let's hide the coins—under chickens and, oh, on windowsills and things. Or slip them under people's doors while they sleep! It's just the kind of thing Robin would do, and it'll help when the baron's tax men come."

The forest looked like an entirely different place from how it looked the night Ellie ran away from the mob. Even the leaves seemed gilded with possibility. She thought of the Greenwood Tree, hiding a whole world inside its arms. You could live in these woods if you knew how to do it.

And she could learn. Her mind started to race. Friar Tuck said he lived alone—what if she could join him at the camp, so he could teach her all he knew? Maybe more of the Merry Men would return as the days went by, and Ellie could be part of them.

*All I've ever wanted is to help people*, she reasoned. *It's all I've been learning to do for the last four years at the abbey—well, that and pray.*

What if this was her path? Not to run, and live as a fugitive for the rest of her life, but to become the next Robin Hood?

She fell silent, lagging behind her laughing friends. The people needed a hero—was it so silly to think she could be it? She realized that the League had moved from the grown-over tunnels and hidden paths they usually took on their hunting trips, back to the more trafficked lanes the villagers walked to collect berries and wild herbs for medicines. She was about to direct them off the path when Jacob stopped short and Ellie ran into his back.

"Hey . . . ," she started, then looked up. Her mouth went dry.

A band of villagers stood on the road ahead, blocking their way.

Ellie knew a mob when she saw one. Hadn't she seen the lynch mob that carried Jack Price away after he attacked the girl who had refused to marry him? Or the one that forced Old Man Cooper to share his grain when he was the only one in town who had any? There were men she recognized, and some she didn't, carrying ropes and pitchforks, their faces dark with anger. One of them carried a longbow, but he didn't know how to hold it.

"Quick. Before they can recognize you," murmured Alice. She looped a hand around Ellie's wrist, and Ralf grabbed the other. They walked her backward off the path, into the trees.

"Hello there!" Jacob called. Ellie could hear the easy smile in his voice. "Are you planning to catch yourself a blackberry with that bow, Master Newgate?"

"There were more of you a minute ago," growled Allan Payne. Peering through the branches, Ellie could see his bald head shining with sweat. She took in the mean shine of his eyes, and the sway in his step that matched that of his companions: These men were drunk.

"No, Master Payne," Margery began. "We were walking through the trees because we heard this is the day Queen Mab does her herb picking. If you time it just right, you can gather the juniper her handmaidens have touched, and make it into a medicine that cures any ailment. Even boils," she said, looking pointedly at Andrew Newgate, whose cheeks were pocked with angry red spots. He glared back.

"Don't you lie to me, Margery Drubber!" An older man moved forward in the pack, his jowls shaking with anger. It was Tom Turner. "We've been patrolling the borders of these woods since the girl ran off, just waiting for her to get hungry. Unless, of course, the wolves got hungry first." He laughed, a raw sound, then put his hand on the knife at his belt. "Now give up the Dray girl. We know she's your friend, and we know you're fool enough to try to hide her."

Ellie's face went hot. Ever since Turner drove off his wife and child, he'd looked for other people to vent his nasty temper on. He'd had no quarrel with Ellie before, but she knew he'd swear up and down he'd seen her dance with the devil, if it gave him a chance to make her as miserable as he was.

*I could run*, Ellie thought. *Like I did before. These drunk old men would never catch up. And if they did . . .* Her bow weighed heavy on her shoulder. But no—why should she run if she hadn't done what she was accused of?

She pulled away from Ralph and Alice, and stepped through the trees onto the path. Her heart was pounding, but she stood square and proud.

"You're looking for me, Tom Turner?" she said.

Margery and Jacob stared at Ellie, their faces full of horror. Tom Turner gave a drunken grin. "Well, well," he said. "Decided to give yourself up, murderer?"

"I'm no murderer," Ellie said loudly. "I would never kill Robin Hood, and you all know it. You also know the baron would peddle any story to get what he wants—and what he wants is to blame someone else for his crime. I didn't kill Robin Hood—he did."

To her dismay, her words seemed to bounce off the men like acorns. Then an idea struck her.

She pulled the silver arrow from her quiver, and a ripple of surprise ran through the mob. "You all know what this is, don't you? It belonged to Robin Hood." At their silence her voice rose desperately. "Friar Tuck himself gave it to me. Because he knows I didn't kill Robin. He was Robin's right-hand man, and he believes me."

Tom Turner narrowed his bloodshot eyes. The rest of the mob stared at the arrow, their faces sour with suspicion. Ralph and Alice had stepped out to join Jacob and Margery, all four of them looking between Ellie and the mob. Fear seeped through Ellie, and she began to wish she had stayed hidden in the trees after all. Ralph's pale face, and the tense expressions of the others, told her they thought the same.

"The keys," Ralph called in a hoarse voice. "Ellie, tell them!"

*Of course!*

She took them from her pocket and jangled them. "Look! These are the keys to the baron's castle. We mean to free Maid Marian!"

To her relief, at this some of the men seemed to soften.

"Is this true, girl?" one said gruffly. Ellie recognized him as John Ward, a man with more children than even he could count.

"Yes. The baron killed Robin, and we're going to save Marian before he kills her, too."

Tom Turner strode slowly toward her. He pointed at the purse hanging from her belt, then jabbed his finger in her face. His breath was foul with liquor, his expression triumphant. "If you're on our side against the baron, Dray, then why are you still carrying his reward?"

For a moment Ellie had no reply. Her mind spun, like a cart's wheels trying to find purchase in mud. "I . . . I didn't want to keep it. But if I had to run, I knew I'd need something—"

"Hear that?" Tom snarled. He grabbed her arm in his gnarled hand. "You don't run if you're innocent, girl. I say we take her back to the village and hang her from the highest tree. For Robin Hood!"

His words broke the tenuous hold Ellie had on the mob. Their voices rose to meet Turner's, tangling into one terrible roar. Terror made Ellie's head go sludgy; for a moment she could only look at Tom's hand around her arm. Then Ralf was running toward her.

"Leave her alone!" Ralf yelled, shoving Tom Turner with both hands. "She's telling the truth!"

Turner snarled as Ellie wrenched herself free. Andrew Newgate, sleeves rolled up over brawny arms, cuffed Ralf on the side of his head. He gave a cry and fell, hitting the ground heavily. Alice launched herself at Newgate, barreling into his stomach. He gave a winded gasp and staggered backward.

Jacob yanked a pitchfork from one of the men and swung it like a scythe, forcing others to run clear. Margery had sprung onto a stump at the edge of the path, from where she loosed arrows into the fray, aiming for the ground. More of the mob had to dance away from them to avoid being hit.

Ellie grabbed Ralf and hauled him to his feet.

"Are you all right?" she gasped—then was jerked violently backward. Allan Payne had wrapped an arm around her neck, squeezing until stars exploded in front of her eyes. She tried to cry out but could only wheeze.

Ralf lunged toward her, clawing at Payne's arm. But Newgate grabbed him in his brawny arms, hauling him away and tossing him on the ground once more.

"Margery," Ralf panted, "use your bow!"

As she thrashed in Payne's grip, Ellie saw Margery had an arrow trained toward her. "It's no good!" Margery cried in dismay. "I'll hit Ellie!"

Tom Turner stalked toward Ellie. Grinning, he ripped

the coin purse and stolen keys from her belt. When he reached into her quiver and took the silver arrow, she struggled all the more against Payne's grip. Hot, frustrated tears welled up in her eyes.

"She's purple as a blackberry," Tom Turner said gleefully. "Don't kill her yet, we've got to do this right."

Payne loosened his grip, and honey-sweet air filled her lungs. She gasped it in, then drove an elbow back into Payne's ribs.

"Stop that," he said, giving her a rough shake. "Or we'll hang you from a *low* tree, and let you die slow."

He laughed, and Turner joined him, but Payne's laugh turned into a gargle when Alice dropped on him suddenly from the trees. She hung awkwardly off his neck, slashing shallowly at him with her hunting knife. With a yelp he dropped Ellie. She fell to the ground and fire seemed to course through her. She rolled clear, springing to her feet, and in the next moment she had an arrow strung to her bow.

"You shouldn't have been so greedy," she snapped, training it on Tom Turner. "You should've taken the bow before you took the gold."

Turner's eyes filled with dumb animal fear. Ellie stepped backward, including Payne and the others in her line of fire. To a man, the mob had frozen at the sight of Robin's bow. Even when it wasn't loaded with a silver arrow, it was the most famous weapon in Nottingham. Alice had slithered off Payne's shoulders and sprinted into the trees. Margery stood behind Ellie, tensed to run or to shoot. Jacob and Ralf flanked their leader.

"Come on!" Alice's voice was sharp and panicked. "Let's go!"

"Wait," Ellie said, still holding her bowstring taut. "We can't go without the keys—and the arrow!"

"Alice is right," panted Ralf. "There are too many of them."

Ellie's frustrated fingers longed to send an arrow straight into Tom Turner's cowardly face—and the ruthlessness of her own thoughts turned her cold. Before the men could gather themselves, she lowered her bow, and the League of Archers fled into the woods.

Angry tears flowed freely down Ellie's face. When Ralf noticed, he took the lead, weaving through the trees until they'd shaken off the few of the mob who'd tried to follow.

Ellie cursed herself as she ran. Why hadn't they run from the mob when they'd had the chance? Now they'd lost everything—their only chance at saving Marian, the coins that meant Ellie could flee if she had to, and Robin's arrow. . . . For twenty years it hadn't left his side, and in just one day she'd let it slip from her grasp.

When she realized Ralf was leading them toward their original destination, the pond, she almost laughed. *What's the point?* she thought darkly.

Then the trees gave way to sky, and the pond was ahead of them, silvery gray and rimmed with rushes. They slowed to a halt at its banks, none of them wanting to speak. Finally Margery broke the silence.

"We can't go back to the village, can we? Not after . . ."

Ellie could hear the words Margery couldn't bring herself to say. *Not after being caught helping you.* "I'm sorry," she said hoarsely.

"It'll be all right." Ralf's voice was falsely bright. "Once we clear your name, we can all go home. It's what we wanted to do anyway."

"And we still have food from the friar," Margery reminded them. "Let's just . . . look for somewhere safe to spend the night."

"Father will worry," Alice said quietly, then stopped speaking when Ralf touched her arm.

Even Jacob looked somber as they found a hidden patch of thick grass beneath a willow tree. They didn't dare make a fire, but ate the cold cooked potatoes and hard bread the friar had given them. Nobody felt like talking. Once the meal was over, they wrapped themselves in their cloaks and lay down. Ellie waited until, one by one, her friends' breaths dipped into the steady rhythm of sleep.

While she waited, staring up into dark branches, she took stock of what little they still had. Robin's bow. A quiver full of red-fletched arrows. Cloaks to sleep in, enough coin to buy a few hot meals at a tavern, but certainly not enough to run away with.

She thought, as ever, *What would Robin do?* But for the first time the words seemed to have no meaning.

And was it even the right question to be asking? Her friends had fought valiantly against the villagers, for her. But what if one of Margery's arrows had slipped into someone's heart? What if Alice's knife had found the big man's throat? Then they'd be killers, same as her. Had Robin ever felt guilty for the trouble he led his men into, or had he always looked toward the horizon, and never back? Ellie shuddered, pulling the cloak tighter against the whispering night air. Her mind tiptoed into ever-darker places. She saw the faces of the villagers twisted in anger and hate, their arms tilting back to throw things at her when she'd stood, helpless, in the cart. The village was miles away, but it might as well be across the seas—she could never go back. And because of her, the rest of the League couldn't either.

Ellie flinched and squeezed her hands into fists when

**LEAGUE OF ARCHERS**

the shame of it hit. Because of her, her friends had lost their homes. Even now Mr. Attwood would be peering into the gloom beyond his door, growing more worried every minute Ralf and Alice didn't come home. Margery's parents needed her to do the butchering, and her sisters needed her to help with the little ones. And Jacob was his parents' only child—how would they feel if he never came home?

Ralf believed they could clear her name, but a terror burned in the core of her, souring her stomach and tormenting her with one thought: What would happen to them if they couldn't?

Ellie surged upward in the dark, too dogged by her thoughts to stay still a moment longer. Quietly she stood and crept out from beneath the willow branches. She walked a way through the woods before realizing her feet were sending her to the last place she'd called home: the abbey. When a scrawny rabbit crossed her path, she shot it. A second, fatter one joined it over her shoulder after she spotted it on the edge of the cleared land just before the abbey wall.

Ellie stood for a moment, staring at the worn stone. Then she found a toehold and heaved herself up and over it, landing softly on the grazing grounds of the abbey's goats.

The abbey was dark but for a candle burning in the

window of the hospital wing. Maybe Sister Joan was inside, moving quietly between beds, touching a hand to a forehead here, tucking in a blanket there. The nun hid her kind heart under such a strict exterior, Ellie had spent her first year at Kirklees half-terrified to be in the same room as her.

*Has Mary Ursula turned her against me too?* she wondered bleakly. No, she decided. No matter what the new abbess did, most of the sisters would remain loyal to Marian—and to Sister Bethan, the only person who could rightly succeed her as mother abbess.

The tiny light of the candle sent a twin warmth flaring up in Ellie's chest. Marian's hospital was still helping people. Perhaps Gregory Carpenter was lying in there now, dreaming of Robin Hood. Ellie might have failed at everything else that day, but at least she could see that Gregory and the other patients had a good meal in the morning.

She hoisted the rabbits over her shoulder and ran fleetly over the grounds to the kitchen door. Gently she lay the rabbits down just outside it, imagining Sister Bethan's face when she found them the next morning. With one last look at the place she'd once called home, she crept back to the wall and into the forest beyond.

# 16

ELLIE'S MOUTH TASTED LIKE WEEK-OLD MEAT the next morning, and her eyes felt hot in their sockets. The League walked in silence to the pond, keeping to the most inhospitable paths. The air held the early-morning smell of rain and distant smoke, and a sliver of moon still clung to the lightening sky.

They were subdued, lost in their own thoughts, until the pond came into sight. Then Ralf broke into a sudden run, and the rest of them followed.

He looked down at the grass as if it were gilded. "It was right here?" he asked, his voice breathless. "This is where Robin stood?" When Ellie nodded, he planted his feet and gazed across the water.

"A duck pond is a funny place to meet a legend," Margery said wonderingly. "I'd sooner picture him on the deck of a pirate ship. Or in a gambling den."

"It was for Marian," Ellie said softly. "They parted ways years ago—I don't know why. But I think he was going to see her. Maybe that's how the baron knew where to find him."

"But how could the baron have known that?" Jacob asked. "Marian had him fooled for years. Could he have had his men tracking Robin? The gamekeeper, maybe?"

Ralf snorted. "That old lead foot? We've outrun him a hundred times, and there's five of us to catch. Robin was the most wanted man in England, and he went free for years."

"Robin was old," Alice said starkly. "Maybe he was just getting slow."

Ralf threw her a dirty look.

"Maybe the baron *did* know the abbess was Maid Marian," Ellie said. "Maybe he'd been staking out the road to the abbey, just waiting for Robin to come back to her." But that didn't sound right either—the baron wasn't a patient man. He'd be the kind of hunter who'd let his arrow fly the moment he spotted the deer.

They combed the ground where Ellie had met Robin, but found nothing. She stood exactly where she'd been that night, trying to think of anything she might've missed. Then, in a flash, she remembered the arrow she'd shot into the trees, sent after Robin's unseen assassin. She gasped sharply and took off running.

"What is it, what did you see?" Alice cried, running behind her.

Ellie charged along the arrow's path, as best she could remember, straight into the forest. She looked around wildly, clinging to a scrap of desperate hope—then she spotted it, embedded almost to the fletching in the trunk of a fir tree.

"My arrow," she said. "Don't move!"

She bent forward at the waist and peered at the ground, hoping to find a footprint or a fallen purse or anything that might hint at who had stood there that night, watching Robin shoot his last duck. But the ground was cloaked with browning pine needles and moldering leaves.

Still, Ellie moved on tiptoes toward the arrow. When she lifted her arm to ease it from the pine, she saw something that made her fingers tingle.

A scrap of purple fabric was caught on its shaft. She realized with a shock how close she'd been to catching Robin's killer that very night—but not close enough. She'd merely shot off a piece of his cloak.

Margery gasped when she saw what Ellie had found. "You were right," she said. "We *did* find a clue."

"Purple," Jacob said sharply. "He must be rich. No poor man would dare wear a royal color, he'd be arrested."

"So the killer can't have been the gamekeeper," pointed out Ralf, "or even a soldier. What if it *was* the baron?"

"If the baron had been here that night, he'd already be dead," Ellie said. "He's so soft and stupid from living in that castle, I'd have skewered him like a rabbit. But I've seen this color before—on the baron's fancy French friend."

"Oh, I remember him," Ralf said, pointing to his still-bruised cheek. It had faded to a sickly yellow color.

"His cloak wasn't torn, I don't think," said Ellie, "and he didn't look like the kind who'd wear it again if it was. But who knows how many Frenchmen the baron's hiding?" The edge of a thought occurred to her then, something that seemed too big to be possible. "What if . . . what if the French king is behind this?" she asked hesitantly.

Alice shook her head doubtfully. "Why would the French care enough about Robin Hood to kill him? If anything, they'd be doing King John a favor."

Knowing she sounded half-crazed, Ellie told them the suspicions she'd first had overhearing the Frenchman and the baron speaking at the castle—that the baron was courting favor with King Philip of France. "He's hedging his bets," she finished darkly. "It doesn't matter if France or England wins the war—he can pretend he was always on the winning side."

Her friends looked slightly stunned when she was done. "Kings and queens have never had much to do with us before," Jacob said dryly. "I think I like them better when they're minding their own business."

"Even if Ellie's right, what would it matter to us if France did win?" Margery said. They all stared at her, but she plowed on. "Oh, come off it. Would it make a lick of difference if we woke up French tomorrow? The sheep would still need to be fed and sheared and butchered. The sun would still rise and fall."

"I think Tom Turner would go after himself with his own pitchfork if he woke up French," Ralf said thoughtfully. "I'd like to see that."

Jacob snorted with laughter. "I still don't see why the French would do King John such a massive favor as killing Robin Hood," he said.

"Maybe they've made a deal," Ellie suggested. "The French kill Robin Hood, and the baron helps King Philip conquer England."

Alice, who'd wandered away while they were talking, snapped her fingers loudly.

"Don't agree with me, Liss?" Ellie asked.

"Probably not, but that's not it—I've found footprints!"

The rest of the League rushed to where she crouched about ten feet past the fir that had held Ellie's arrow. Now Ellie could see what she'd missed before: a slender tunnel of broken branches and trampled grass where the person she'd nearly shot had escaped into the dark. She could just barely make out the imprint of a foot in the damp grass between two trees.

Alice was ahead of them, crouched low over the ground.

"She's as good as the gamekeeper's dog," Jacob muttered.

They followed her as she wove through the woods, crowing over signs they couldn't see until they were pointed out. Then she stopped and snapped upright, frowning.

"Here," she said, pointing down. "The gait changes here—something happened."

The League fanned out through the bushes surrounding the assassin's track. Ellie wasn't sure what she should be looking for until she found it, and yelled out in triumph.

Carefully she freed it from the bushes where it nestled: another arrow, but not her own. It was the twin to the one that had ended the life of Robin Hood. And next to it, snagged against the leaves, a fawn-colored glove, its fingers stained with something dark. The sight of it made the blood beat behind her eyes. Here it was—the proof she'd longed for. But finding it just made her feel sick. This was the escape route of Robin Hood's killer, which meant somewhere in the world he was still alive. And free.

"Look," she said as her friends gathered around her. "The glove's covered with poison, I bet."

"Don't touch it with your bare hands," Margery said sharply. Ellie nodded, using a stick to pull it loose. Ralf held out his cap, and Ellie carefully flipped the glove into the bowl of it.

"Do you recognize the arrow?" Ellie asked Jacob. His fletcher father made it his business to buy from other fletchers for miles around, to pick up their tricks and satisfy himself that his own arrows were best.

Jacob peered at the arrow, then gingerly lifted it to study the fletching. "I don't," he said finally. "It's very distinctive, though—my father might recognize it if I show it to him. Or he'll at least know if it's French-made. I'll ask him as soon as he's back from Nottingham."

Alice had already burrowed ahead, following the altered path. Suddenly she stopped short.

"It ends here," she said, her face looking betrayed. "The tracks disappear into thin air!"

Margery let out a strangled cry. "What if it's a ghost?" she said.

"Ghosts don't wear purple cloaks and shoot poisoned arrows," Ellie said. "He can't have just *flown* away—are you sure you're not missing his tracks?"

Alice glared at her. "Remind me, who tracked Friar Tuck all the way to the Greenwood Tree? I'm telling you, the footprints end."

"Maybe he climbed a tree?" Ralf said doubtfully. They looked up at the trees where Alice stood, all of them too thin for even Alice to climb.

"Not possible," Jacob said. "Not even our mysterious French assassin could scale those things."

"Hey, you—this is the baron's land!"

The gamekeeper's harsh voice cut through the air. They hadn't heard his approach, but now the sound of him and his black dog crashing through the trees filled Ellie with cold fear.

"Run!" she gasped.

They took off, but the gamekeeper was too close—this time he'd catch them. She could feel it.

"We have to split up," she called. "Weave through the trees!"

An arrow whizzed over her shoulder, turning her blood to ice.

"Shoot him, Ellie," Jacob cried from behind her. "You're the best shot!"

Ellie kept running, shaken by indecision. With Robin's bow she was certain she could hit him. But what if he died? Could she hold her head up with two men's deaths on her hands?

*I wouldn't shoot his dog,* she thought as she ran. *And the gamekeeper is no more guilty—he's just another of the baron's bloodhounds.*

At the same time the old question came back to her: What would Robin Hood do? And with a cold clarity she knew the answer. If she were Robin Hood, the gamekeeper would already have an arrow through his heart.

Then Ralf screamed, pitching hard to the ground. Ellie skidded to a stop, dropping beside him. Bright blood ran down his neck, and his eyes were wild.

Ellie's fingers found the place where the gamekeeper's arrow had grazed across his cheek. "It's just a scratch," she soothed. "You'll be fine."

Had it struck a finger's length over, Ralf would be dead. Ellie rose to her feet on a wave of rage. By the time the gamekeeper's scowling face was in her sights, she had an arrow on her bow, aimed at his heart.

*No. I can't do it.*

She swung the bow to the right and released the string. Her arrow slid neatly into the gamekeeper's hand.

He bellowed with pain, dropping his bow and clutching the wounded hand to his chest.

"Can you run?" Jacob asked Ralf urgently, crouching beside him. Ralf nodded, but when he tried to stand, his knees buckled. Jacob grabbed him up and slung him over his shoulder.

"Keep your hand pressed to the wound!" Margery cried as they ran from the gamekeeper. He started to rush after them but then seemed to think better of it, sending a volley of curses at their speeding backs.

When they finally stopped, Ralf's face was the color of new milk.

"I'm fine," he mumbled as Margery sopped up the blood with a strip of fabric Ellie had cut from her cloak.

"It's a nice, clean wound," Margery said, eyeing it with an expert's air. "It'll heal up straight if you keep it clean. If I can just find some yarrow, that should do you for now."

"And now you'll have a scar," Jacob said helpfully. "Every one of the Merry Men has a dozen scars at least."

Ralf nodded, but his gaze was unfocused. Ellie's and Alice's eyes met nervously, then darted away.

Looking for a distraction, Ellie pulled the cap that held the poisoned glove from Ralf's sack. "You're so good at telling herbs apart," she said. "Can you give this a sniff? Maybe you can figure out what was used in the poison."

Ralf dipped his head carefully toward the glove, then recoiled. "Ugh. It's disgusting. Are you sure that thing's an herb?"

Ellie smiled with relief at the weak joke. Ralf sniffed the glove again, then shook his head.

"I can't smell anything under the rottenness. You'll need someone more expert than me."

She'd brought out the glove only to take Ralf's mind from his wound, but now she was really curious. Maybe identifying the poison—or the ingredients in it—would illuminate something for them, some clue they couldn't see. "You're right," she said. "And I think I know who might be able to help."

# 17

THE ABBEY LOOKED DIFFERENT IN THE SUN-
light as the League approached its western wall. Colder.
Maybe it was the idea of Mother Mary Ursula awake and
moving through its halls, poisoning the air with her
entitlement and her whisperings. Marian, Ellie realized,
had been the abbey's heart. It wouldn't be the same
without her.

She led the League to the place where the wall was
lowest, to the pushed-out stone she'd scrambled over
last night, with the crab apple tree that formed a handy
ladder on the other side.

"We mustn't let anyone see us," she breathed. "I
don't want to get anyone in trouble—and if Sister Mary

Ursula thinks any of the sisters have helped me, they'll be punished. Who knows what she's made the other nuns believe about me? But I know we can trust Sister Bethan. She'll be somewhere in the garden."

Jacob started to grab a handhold on the wall, but Ellie pulled him back. "Boys can't go in there! That's a nunnery!"

Jacob grinned. "Oh yeah."

Ellie climbed over the wall, just as she'd done so many times before. But this time her heart was beating as fast as a butterfly's wings. She crouched in the thin cover of the crab apple's branches for a moment, surveying the grounds. When nobody came into view, she dropped to the grass. Moments later Margery and Alice climbed down beside her.

The three girls huddled in the shade. "Okay," Ellie said quietly, pulling her cloak up around her head. "Stay close to me, and don't let yourself be seen."

That was easier said than done. The abbey's rolling grounds were verdant green, broken up by garden beds and outbuildings and spindly fruit trees. Ellie decided their safest bet was to keep close to the walls, so they could scramble back over if spotted.

As they skirted the edge of the abbey's small orchard, she spied Novice Agnes and Sister Margery gathering apples, spinning them in their hands to check for squirrel bites. Sister Ethel oversaw their labor, leaning drowsily against a tree trunk and eating a piece of bright-fleshed fruit.

The sweet, cidery smell of rotting fruit and the sight of the novices in their robes sent a pang through Ellie. It wasn't homesickness exactly—it was more a feeling of regret that she could never go back to this life. Such a quiet existence would never have been enough for her, but she still regretted losing it.

"Is one of them Sister Bethan?" whispered Margery.

Ellie shook her head. "Let's try the kitchen garden."

Alice's eyes widened. "Kitchen garden . . . as in, right next to the kitchen? In the middle of the day?"

"We've come this far, Liss," Margery said. "May as well see it through."

When the nuns turned to pile the apples into a basket, Ellie led the girls in a sprint to a tumbledown barn midway between the wall and the abbey. She wrinkled her nose as powdery lichen from its sides came off on her hands. At her signal they ran again, this time stopping behind a stone woodshed. She waited a long moment— for a shout, some signal they'd been seen—then peered carefully around the building's side.

Sister Bethan was in the garden. Her familiar shape, rounded and comfortable beneath her robes, made Ellie's eyes hot with unshed tears. She longed to run forward and throw her arms around the old woman—but Sister Bethan wasn't alone. Sister Mary Francis stood some way off, wringing her hands. The reason for her distress was clear: Mother Mary Ursula stood beside Sister Bethan, proud and thin lipped in the robes of an abbess.

Ellie's heart leaped into her throat. She shushed Alice and Margery, straining to hear the women's conversation.

"They're just novices," Sister Bethan was saying, the anger in her voice barely held in check. "Their hands are too cut up from your lashes for them to do their chores. The mother abbess would never have used such harsh punishment. Not for such a small trespass."

"Ah, but I *am* the mother abbess," Mother Mary Ursula replied coldly. "I don't believe I've heard you address me as such even once."

Sister Bethan looked at the ground. "It's so new a thing," she said through gritted teeth. "If you would . . . Reverend Mother, please allow Sister Joan to make a poultice for their hands. I'll tend to them myself. I assure you they won't be caught sneaking food again after this."

"So you do see the wisdom of my ways! I've punished them once, and saved you years of kitchen thefts in the future." Mother Mary Ursula paused. "They cannot do their chores, you say? Everyone must carry her weight under my roof. But I'm not a cruel woman—you can tend to their hands after final prayers."

Sister Bethan barely nodded in response, and Ellie burned with anger.

Gesturing at Sister Mary Francis to follow her, Mother Mary Ursula turned and walked back toward the abbey. Ellie hated the thought of her sleeping in the abbess's chamber, running her white hands over the abbess's possessions. Hurting novices because she could. Ellie made herself wait until Mother Mary Ursula was out of sight, then another minute longer, before running toward Sister Bethan.

When the old nun saw Ellie, her whole body went taut. Then she was running toward her. They met in a hard hug, one that smelled of rosemary and bread dough.

"Sister Bethan, I—"

"Elinor Dray!" She leaned back and pressed a kiss on Ellie's forehead. "We worried you were dead, but those rabbits told me otherwise. You're a good girl. I knew you wouldn't forget us, any more than we'd forget you. Now what in the world are you doing here?"

"I wanted—"

"If Sister Mary Ursula sees you, you'll be in worse trouble than you think." Sister Bethan glanced at Margery and Alice, who were waiting beside Ellie. "Your friends, too. She'll have you all locked up before you can say—"

"We had to come," Ellie burst out. "We need your help."

She explained about the townspeople believing the baron's lies, and the glove she thought might prove her innocence. "We just need to know what the poison is made of. What if it can be matched to something French—some herb that grows only on their soil? It could be enough to clear my name, prove the baron had a hand in it! If everyone knows he's guilty, we'll have a chance of freeing the abbess!"

Sister Bethan smiled sadly. "I'll look at your poison, but I think it will take an act of God to bring back the abbess. Even if the baron is guilty, he'll worm out of it somehow. The man is as slippery as an eel."

She looked around quickly, then led the girls back behind the shed. "I can't be gone long," she said. "Sister Mary Francis has the nerves of a butterfly, she'll think I've been kidnapped. Now let me see that glove."

Ellie pulled it from her sleeve and carefully unrolled the hat that held it.

"Ugh," said the old nun, touching a hand to her nose. "This stinks of the devil—sulfur and blood."

She dared another sniff, dipping her head delicately toward the glove. "That stench! This is no Christian poison, Ellie. Not that there's any such thing." After narrowing her eyes and shifting the glove in the light, she shook her head. "I'm afraid I can't tell you what's in that horrible brew, not just from smelling it. It's beyond my powers."

"But . . . we came all this way," Ellie said, hating the pleading note in her voice.

Sister Bethan's gaze turned shrewd. "You're brave, Elinor Dray, but you're not looking far enough ahead. What if you find this *is* a French poison? What then? Declare war on all of France?"

Ellie knew there was wisdom in Sister Bethan's words, but . . . "I can't just give up," Ellie protested. "The mother abbess has nobody but me to help her. I don't care what happens to me now, so long as the baron doesn't get away with this."

The nun watched her a moment, then nodded. "Spoken like Maid Marian herself." Again she threw a quick glance to both sides, then leaned in closer. "You know my place is here, within the abbey's walls. And I cannot condone violence. But there are some who, like you, would go to any length to save the abbess's life—and I believe God is on their side. And justice, too."

From the other side of the shed came Sister Mary Francis's voice, calling for Sister Bethan.

The old nun bent forward and grabbed Ellie's hands. "May you find those allies, Elinor Dray. May you live to serve justice, and walk free." She dropped a kiss on

Ellie's forehead. "And may God bless you all. Now *go*."

Ellie, Margery, and Alice did as she said, making straight for the wall. As she ran, Ellie heard Sister Bethan bustling back to the garden, distracting the younger nun so they could make their getaway.

Nobody saw them racing for the wall but a skinny gray rabbit, which froze in place, watching them with a beady eye. On the other side they found the boys stuffing their mouths with the mulberries that grew along the wall.

"You're back quick!" Ralf said, his mouth stained red.

"We've hit a dead end," Ellie sighed. "Sister Bethan supports us, but she can't help us. God knows what we should do next."

"Well." Margery looked a bit shifty. "I might have one more idea."

Ralf raised his eyebrows. "What's that, then?"

"I didn't want to say so in front of the sister," said Margery, "but when she said that thing, about it being no Christian poison? Well, I thought of someone who might know something about all sorts of *un*-Christian things. Her name is Mother Barkbone, and she lives outside the village."

Ellie's heart sank. She'd heard of Mother Barkbone—every child in the village had. Some said she was a witch. When Ellie was tiny, their neighbor Helen Pygott had said that if Ellie stole any more of her strawberries, she'd send her to old Mother Barkbone to grind up her bones for a love draft. When Ellie told her mother, she laughed. Mother Barkbone made harmless remedies, she said, and Helen Pygott was daft to believe otherwise.

But Jacob's eyes were wide. "The Mother Barkbone who cursed William Croft's chickens to lay scrambled eggs? Isn't she more likely to turn us into goats than to help us?"

"Oh, you sound like Tom Turner," Margery snapped. "People from the village go to her all the time. And she won't care a bit what Tom or anyone else thinks of you, Ellie, because she doesn't think much of the village."

The League was looking at Ellie eagerly, waiting her decision. Inwardly she groaned. How could Mother Barkbone, of all people, be their only hope of uncovering Robin's murderer? But it was the only plan they had.

She forced herself to smile as brightly as she could. "What are we waiting for? Let's see what Mother Barkbone has to say."

# 18

MOTHER BARKBONE'S COTTAGE WAS ABOUT A mile north of the village. If Ellie weren't a fugitive, she and her friends could take a wide footpath lined with tangled honeysuckles halfway there, then duck onto a narrow turning that led straight to the old woman's door. As it was, they trudged through a stretch of thick woods instead. They were overheated and grumpy by the time the forest spat them out into the tiny clearing surrounding Mother Barkbone's cottage.

The tumbledown structure looked half-reclaimed by trees. The whole thing was made of slumped gray stone, the bottom of it overgrown with butter-colored wildflowers. Vines wound in and around a crumbling chimney, and the thatched roof looked like the flank of a balding animal. No sound came from the cottage, and the door was shut tight, but Ellie had the uncomfortable feeling of being watched. Witch or not, she wasn't looking forward to stepping inside Mother Barkbone's home.

"Well, Marge," said Jacob. "Do the honors?"

Margery heaved a big breath and walked forward with short, halting steps. The rest of the League gathered behind her as she knocked softly on the cottage's rough wooden door.

Almost immediately a voice as creaky as a cellar door called out to them. "Come in!"

*So we* were *being watched*, Ellie thought. She squared her shoulders and calmed her breathing. *You've faced off against the baron's guards and two angry mobs*, she told herself. *Who are you to be scared of an old herb wife?*

Margery pushed open the door, and the five of them stepped over the threshold. Then Ellie nearly screamed at the feeling of something soft and insistent pressing itself against her ankles.

It was a small, cloud-colored cat with peering green eyes like washed river stones. The rest of the cottage was even stranger. It was so full of plants, both growing from pots and hanging upside down to dry, that Ellie had the momentary illusion she'd stepped through the door and right back into the forest. She stifled a gasp when she came face-to-face with a stuffed water rat, hung from the ceiling. More cats prowled around their ankles, all of them sharing the same spooky-colored eyes.

"Be welcome, children," said the creaky voice, this time much closer. From a dark corner of the cottage, where the walls bristled with hanging herbs and glass bottles full of shriveled dead things, appeared Mother Barkbone.

She was ancient, older even than the oldest nun at Kirklees. Her face was as wizened as oak bark, but the eyes peering from it were bright. Ellie's heart did a funny hop—the woman had the same eerie green gaze as her cats.

The woman took Margery's hand and smiled, her wrinkles folding in on one another. "It's lovely to see you, dear. How is your mother?"

"Much better, Mother Barkbone," Margery said respectfully. "She says she doesn't know what she'd do without your herbs."

The woman smiled and patted Margery's cheek. Then her gaze shifted past her and fell on Ellie. She dropped Margery's hand, and her strange eyes bore into Ellie's. Mother Barkbone lurched forward and grabbed her by the wrist.

Her grip was shockingly strong for such an old woman; for one wild moment Ellie feared she couldn't pull free.

"I would read your fortune," the old woman said.

Ellie shifted uncomfortably. "I was a novice, Mother Barkbone," she said. "Thank you, but I don't believe in such things."

The woman shrugged. "Believe or don't believe, but listen at least."

"We're not here for that. We need your help with something, it's very important—"

Ellie winced as the woman's grip grew tighter. "I'll help you, child, but first you'll let me tell you your fortune."

"But isn't that . . ." Ellie struggled to speak politely. "Is fortune-telling not a tool of the devil, Mother Barkbone?" she finished awkwardly. For a moment she had a discomforting flash of Mother Mary Ursula agreeing heartily with her words.

Rather than being offended, the old woman laughed. The cats scattered at the sound, one of them taking a swipe at Ralf's ankle before disappearing into the cottage's half-dead sea of greenery.

"The devil and I walk different byways," she said. "I respect his power just as I respect that of God's. But I worship the things I can see, the spirits who speak back to me. Those of the land, those of my ancestors. They guide me true and would never lead me into the devil's mouth. You're safer from him here than out there, I would wager."

Everything the woman said seemed oceans away from

the mother abbess and her jeweled Bible, the comforting evening hymns laid out in straight lines of ink. But now the old witch was dragging Ellie to a rutted wood table. She swept her arm across it, clearing it of scattered herbs, and reached into the pouch around her neck.

Mother Barkbone cast a handful of dry brown bones across the tabletop. The League, watching eagerly from the doorway, the hissing cats, even the dank blood-and-lavender smell of the cottage, faded away as she looked deep into Ellie's face, then down at the bones.

"How interesting," she muttered. "Just as I expected."

Despite herself a curiosity seized hold of Ellie—she needed to know what the old herb wife saw in the arrangement of bones. She squeezed back when Mother Barkbone gripped her hands.

"Do not fear the wolf, child," she said. Her creaky voice sounded richer somehow, wound through with a sorrowful bass note that hadn't been there before. "You could waste many lifetimes trying to outrun it, but the wolf will follow you for the rest of your life." Mother Barkbone's hands twisted so tightly around Ellie's the bones in them popped. "But you must not be afraid. If you could see its face, you'd see nothing but yourself looking back. You're not meant to be the lamb, my daughter. Your destiny, always, is to be the wolf."

The wolf . . . or the wolf's-head. It was another word for outlaw, because men like the baron would pursue outlaws to the death, just like they would a wolf. Mother Barkbone dropped Ellie's hands and pitched forward onto the table, gasping.

"Mother Barkbone?" Ellie breathed.

The old woman went utterly still, then looked up at Ellie. "Did you like your fortune, child?"

Ellie ignored the question, shaking the fog from her head. *It's nonsense*, she told herself. *And it's not why we're here.*

"You said you'd help us if I let you read my fortune." Ellie fumbled the glove back out of her sleeve, letting it drop to the table beside the bones. "We need to know what's in this poison. We took it to the—to a friend, and she could only identify sulfur. And blood. Can you tell us anything more about it?"

"Of course I can," said Mother Barkbone. "After all, I was the one who brewed it."

Ellie stared at her. The League was speechless, until Ralf burst out, "That's the poison that killed Robin Hood! Who'd you sell it to?"

The old woman cocked her head, her eye as bright as a bird's. "Why, I made it for the hooded man himself. Otherwise known as Robin Hood. He paid me more than most do." From a pocket she drew out a gleaming gold coin engraved with the profile of King John.

Ellie frowned. "Are you sure it was Robin?" None of it made sense. "How could the baron kill him with his own poison?"

Mother Barkbone put the gold coin back in her pocket. "It was him," she said. "And I'm sorry to hear the stories of his death are true."

Ralf was growing red with anger. "It's not true!" he cried. "Robin Hood would never use poison. Poison's for cowards who don't want to fight. Besides, he never killed anybody."

Mother Barkbone broke into a hacking cackle.

"Do you really believe that bedtime story? You're young, dear, but you're not that young. Robin and his Merry Men killed hundreds over the years. And they were right to do so—much blood must be spilled to turn the tide."

Margery cast a worried look at Ralf then asked Mother Barkbone, "But are you certain it was Robin who bought the poison? Could it have been some other outlaw?"

Mother Barkbone scoffed. "I know a wolf when I see one." The words, and the quick glance she cast at her, sent a shiver through Ellie.

The old woman turned back to Ralf, who looked as if he were about to cry. "Dead is dead," she said more gently, "and the acts of the dead are not for us to judge.

But when you're looking for a man's killer, you might start by looking at the man himself."

She gathered the folds of her cloak around her, settling into them like a cat laying itself down in front of a fire. "That's all I can tell you. I'm weary now, and wish to be alone."

The League looked at one another, not one of them satisfied. Finally Margery stepped forward and took the woman's hand. "Thank you, Mother Barkbone. For the fortune, and the advice."

"Give your mother my best wishes, dear." The old woman's voice was creakier than ever, and her strange gaze looked far away.

They trooped outside in silence, not speaking again until they'd reached the safety of the woods.

"She's talking nonsense," Ralf exploded. "How could Robin have had a hand in his own death? Sorry, Marge, but that mad old woman told us nothing!"

His words were angry, but his voice sounded desperate. He wanted so badly to believe what he was saying.

Ellie wished more than anything that she could agree with him. But despite her doubts about Mother Barkbone, she couldn't dismiss what the old woman had said. Not the fortune, and not her advice about Robin Hood. What if he hadn't been killed for being an outlaw? What if his death had something to do with Robin himself?

# 19

ELLIE COULDN'T BRING HERSELF TO PUT those thoughts into words. Ralf looked miserable, and Margery kept glancing at her with concern in her eyes—or pity, over what the old witch thought Ellie's future would hold. *Am I really meant to live like a wolf—like an outlaw?* Ellie wondered. She couldn't think any further ahead than proving her innocence. But what if Mother Barkbone was right? What if it was her destiny?

"Well, what next?" Jacob asked her, smiling faintly and dipping into an exaggerated bow. "We're at your service."

She wished for a moment that they weren't. She'd always led the League, but never like this. Every step they took brought new danger, disappointment, or compromise. And they never seemed any closer to saving Maid Marian.

"The poison doesn't make any sense," she said. "But we still have the arrow. Maybe we can try to find out who made it."

"My father should be back from Nottingham by now," Jacob offered. "We could show it to him . . ." He cut off suddenly, his face flushed.

"We can't go back," Margery reminded him softly. "It's too dangerous."

"What if we go in disguise?" Ellie asked.

"Putting a horse blanket over your head isn't the trick to everything," Alice said.

Ralf snapped his fingers. "We'll go the back way, sneak onto our farm from the woods. There'll be something in the house we can use to hide our faces."

Ellie could tell Alice and Margery remained unconvinced, but nobody had a better idea. They walked to the place where the forest ended in a long stretch of scrubland, running into the end of Ralf and Alice's family's farm. The sun felt good and hot on Ellie's face as they stepped into open air. They passed the place where the cottage had stood, the one Ellie was meant to live in with her mother. The grass was beginning to grow back in. Ralf saw her looking and slung an arm over her shoulders. She let her head touch his for just a moment, gratefully.

The distant sound of shouts reached them; in the shadow of the house little Henry and Matilda Attwood were playing some game that involved taking turns whacking each other with sticks, then flopping down in the grass and pretending to be dead.

When Matilda saw them coming, she sprang to her feet, taking off over the field with her little brother at her heels.

But when she came close enough to see Ellie, she slowed to a halt. Matilda put one foot on top of the other and threw an arm out to hold her brother behind her. The mistrustful look on her face made Ellie want to cry.

"Hey." Ralf crouched down and held out his arms. "You don't believe any of that silly stuff you've heard about Ellie, do you?"

Matilda started to nod, then stopped.

"You know Ellie," he reminded her. "She'd never hurt a hero like Robin."

Finally Matilda dropped her arm, letting Henry come out from behind her. "Okay," she said, her voice a grave echo of Alice's. "I believe you."

She shook hands with Ellie shyly, then looked awed

when Ellie let her hold Robin's bow. It looked huge in her hands.

"Did you come back to fight them?" she asked, pretending to shoot an arrow across the field. "Everyone who thinks you killed Robin?"

"Not yet," Ellie said. "First we're going to try something else—and we need really good disguises to do it. Can you help us?"

The girl considered it a moment, then ran into the house. When she returned, she was holding an armful of clothes. Ralf and Alice looked stricken when they saw them—aside from a couple of old caps of Master Attwood's, they used to belong to their mother. Even for Ellie the clothes conjured up an image of the woman as she'd been when she was alive. Skinny and strong, like Alice, with a big laugh and thick, wheat-colored hair she kept plaited tight against her head.

They took turns ducking into the barn to change. Ellie pulled a rough shift over her own clothes. It was too big, but she tied it up with a belt and then topped it off with a hooded cloak.

Before rejoining her friends, she watched them for a moment from the shadows of the barn. They were neglecting everything to help her. Their families, their work. Who knew how angry Master Attwood was with his children right now, and with her? *As soon as we trace this back to the baron, we can return to our normal lives,* she thought. She could almost make herself believe it too. If she forgot about the old woman's prophecy.

When Ellie left the barn, Margery tilted her head and smiled.

"You look completely the wrong shape, Ellie. I'd never know it was you, not if I didn't see your face." Margery had a blanket around her shoulders and a bonnet that cast her face in shadow. Grudgingly Jacob had pulled on another one of Mistress Attwood's faded dresses, and now he wouldn't stop curtsying.

They decided to enter the village in pairs—Ralf and Alice, then Jacob and Margery. Finally, Ellie would walk alone to meet them at Jacob's house. Before they left, Matilda brought them fried bread left over from the morning.

Twenty minutes later the food lurched in Ellie's stomach as she contemplated walking through the village on her own. Her friends should be at the Galpins' house already. She decided to focus just on her destination and walk, hoping for the best.

Right before she left, she had a flash of genius. She ducked back inside the barn and grabbed a bowl used for grain from the ground, put it under her dress, and rested one hand on it. Then she pulled her hood around her face and walked out the door with a pregnant woman's waddle.

As she walked, blinking, past houses where women washed potatoes and grubby children played in the dirt, she wondered if her pretend belly was drawing more attention to her, rather than less.

But the villagers' gazes seemed to slide right off her. Martha Ward, a baby in one arm and a bucket in the other, looked at her with faint suspicion, then was distracted by the baby's squalls. Ellie's heart beat faster when she saw old Edmund Cole, but he grunted a greeting at Martha and kept walking. They took her for a stranger, with child and wearing a faded dress. They were worried she might be looking for a coin or a handout, and were glad enough to ignore her when she didn't ask.

By the time Ellie reached the town square, where Jacob's sturdy, wooden-framed house and his father's fletcher's shop stood, her stomach was slippery with sweat—from heat rather than fear—beneath the bowl. The Galpins' horse, Juniper, pulled up mouthfuls of grass out front. Ellie smiled and quickened her step.

The sudden sight of Tom Turner made her remember to be afraid. The old man leaned against the wall of his shabby house, not half the size of the Galpins' home, drinking from a smeared tankard. The sun was still a ways above the horizon, but she could see him already swaying on his feet as she scurried past.

An idea struck her then, a bright, formless thing that made her sneak one last look back at Turner. She had no time to stop, so she tucked the thought away for later.

Jacob answered the door nearly the moment she began to knock. His worried expression dissolved into laughter when he saw her stomach. He laughed even harder when she let the bowl fall to her feet.

"Well, it worked, didn't it?" she said, laughing. Her laughter faded to quiet when she looked behind Ralf.

The League was there—but Jacob's parents were too. His mother sitting at the table, her expression unreadable, and his father looming over her anxiously.

"It's all right," Jacob said quickly. "They believe you. They would never take the baron's word over yours."

His mother nodded agreement. "And we're ready to hide you too. Just for a few days, until we can make plans to get you out of the county. I have a sister in Nottingham who you might be able to go to—I can take you there, ask her to let you stay for a while."

"That's very kind, Mistress Galpin. But I have no intention of leaving. I'm going to find out who really killed Robin." She looked at Jacob's dad imploringly. "Sir, I just hope you'll help me do it."

Galpin nodded hesitantly. He was a tall man with thinning red-blond hair and a high forehead that made him look like an egg. Ellie had always found him kind enough, though distracted. But now he looked as if he were having trouble breathing.

*I can't blame him for not wanting a fugitive in his house,* she thought.

Jacob unpacked the arrow they'd found. Its appearance only seemed to make Galpin more nervous, and he barely looked at it before dropping back into a chair. "I don't remember every arrow I've ever seen," he said. "You can't expect that, can you?"

"But, Father," Jacob pleaded, "can't you try?"

Galpin ignored his son, taking a deep drink of mead from the tankard his worried wife pressed into his hands.

"Just look one more time, if you could," Ellie said. "Anything you can think of might help us discover who killed Robin Hood."

At her last words the man's hand twitched, sending his tankard crashing to the floor. The mead pooled around his feet. He slumped forward, catching his head in his hands.

"I cannot keep it to myself," he said, his voice as bumpy as if he were traveling over a hard road. "I must confess. It was all my fault—I killed Robin Hood."

# 20

IN THE SHOCKED SILENCE THAT FOLLOWED, Jacob let out a choked cry.

"It's not what it sounds like," his mother said hurriedly, laying a hand on her husband's shoulder. "George, you need to tell them everything."

Master Galpin breathed deeply, running a hand down his face. "It was less than a month ago. A man came to my shop one night, very late. He asked me to make arrows unlike any I'd made before—arrows that would be untraceable, he said. That's when I knew he'd be using them for something lawless—but fool that I am, I thought it had to do with rebellion." He looked around at them imploringly. "So I made him a clutch of beautiful red-fletched arrows, akin to something I'd seen in London, but of my own design. He paid me well for them—too well. I knew when he handed over his gold that he was paying not just for the arrows but my silence."

*Gold?* Ellie sat straighter. Few people who came through their village had gold to spend—fewer still, she imagined, gave gold to Mother Barkbone. Yet it was used to purchase both the arrows and the poison.

"Days later the baron came into town with . . . with Robin's body. Lying broken in that cart. And when he showed us the arrow that killed him, I saw it was *my* arrow." He shuddered, his eyes staring at some far-off point, as if seeing the dead outlaw before him. "I didn't know what to do. All I could think was, *I've killed Robin Hood.* Even if I didn't shoot the arrow, it was me who made the murder weapon."

He reached desperately toward Ellie, his eyes tearful. "And you, how you must despise me. I was a coward. I let you take the blame, even when I knew you didn't do it. But I'll do anything now, anything to help you get free of this."

A strange mix of pity and anger surged through Ellie, making her feel sick. Master Galpin might not have shot the arrow, but there was no doubt he nearly let Ellie hang for it.

She swallowed. Losing her temper woul

"Describe the man who bought the arrows,

stiffly. "Tell me everything you remember."

Galpin nodded rapidly. "He was a tall man, older than me but not old. His hair was brown and hung to his shoulders, but his cheeks were clean shaven. And this I can't forget—he wore a purple cloak. Not a color you often see in the village."

*A purple cloak!*

"And his accent," Ellie said, her heart beginning to speed up. "It was French, wasn't it?"

But Master Galpin shook his head. "French? No, he was a local man, I'd say. At least by the sound of his voice."

The words hit Ellie like a bucket of cold river water. "You're sure of it? Could he have disguised his speech perhaps, twisted it to make himself sound English?"

"He could join a company of players if that were so," Galpin said. "He was a Nottinghamshire man, I'm certain."

Ellie turned away. If the assassin wasn't one of the baron's Frenchmen, who could it be? *Maybe he paid someone to buy the arrows*, she thought. *And loaned them a cloak!* She shook her head in disgust—it was too fanciful. She felt more hopeless than ever. Each time she thought they

.ere getting somewhere, they ended up further from the truth than before.

She shot a look at her friends. Ralf, Alice, and Margery looked as hangdog as she felt. Jacob just stared at the floor, misery pulling down the sides of his mouth.

There was a rapid knocking at the door. Everyone started.

"No one must see her!" Mistress Galpin whispered.

Jacob grabbed Ellie's arm and bundled her into the next room, where a cauldron of stew simmered over a glowing fire. He slipped away and Ellie heard the door open.

"Have you heard the news?" It was Catherine Baker, her voice was high and out of breath. Ellie knew she had a nose for gossip and relished spreading bad news.

"Catherine! What news, dear?" asked Mistress Galpin.

Ellie heard Catherine gasp. "Jacob is here! With his friends, too. I should've known that fool Tom Turner was lying when he said you were helping that dreadful Dray girl. How relieved I am!" But her voice sounded distinctly disappointed.

"What was your news, Catherine?" Mistress Galpin tried again, her voice a little shrill.

"Oh! The abbess—Maid Marian—was called to trial!"

Ellie sank down beside the fire, pressing her hands to her mouth.

"She had no family left to speak for her, poor thing, and she wouldn't deny a word of the baron's charges. She admitted to all of it—aiding the poor against the baron's wishes, trying to save Robin's life." Catherine stopped and took a ragged breath. "She told the truth, and it has cost her dearly. She'll be hanged tomorrow at dawn."

The words rang in Ellie's ears. Maid Marian—hanged—tomorrow! Ellie remembered the abbey, how cold and strange it had looked with the abbess no longer inside it. If Maid Marian was killed, would the whole world feel that way to her? Colder, because one of the people she loved best was no longer in it?

*I can't let it happen*, she thought. *I can't.*

Catherine Baker was crying now. Mistress Galpin made soothing noises, but Ellie could hear the impatience in her voice. She wanted to get her out of the house.

Ellie heard the creak of Master Galpin's chair. "Let's go and talk to the Wards," he suggested. "They'll want to know. John Ward saw Robin shoot once, years ago. At an archery contest."

When the door had closed behind them, Ellie rushed back to the front room. Ralf had his arm around Alice, and Jacob looked as if he might cry. Margery was flopped down miserably on a chair.

"We have to save Marian," Ellie said fervently.

"You've been saying that and saying that," Alice said sharply. "But nothing we do seems to work."

"Shut it, Liss," Ralf growled. "We *will* save her, but we can't do it alone—we need to find the rest of the Merry Men! Let's go back to the Greenwood Tree and talk to Friar Tuck again. We'll get Marian clear of the baron and everything will be all right!"

The foolish hope shining in his eyes made Ellie want to scream. "The Merry Men aren't coming, Ralf. The Merry Men were never going to come."

He looked at her, his smile slipping and his face closing like a fist. But she couldn't stop.

"We should've listened to Friar Tuck in the first place—Robin's men don't care about him anymore. And why should they? By all accounts he was a foolish, selfish man. A man who led his friends into danger." The words stuck in her throat like a fish bone, but she charged on. "A man who killed many, helped a few, and then disappeared for years. He even abandoned Marian!"

"You can't mean that," Ralf said sadly. "You know Robin was a hero."

"I don't. I know almost nothing about him. But I do know about *Marian*. I know she's good, and brave, and noble. I know she'd do anything to help anyone with less than they needed. And I know that nobody is coming to save her tomorrow if we don't do it."

The door swung open with a startling suddenness, and Catherine Baker stood on the threshold. "Jacob, do you have a cup of water you can spare . . . ," she began. Then her eyes fell on Ellie. For a moment she froze. Before Ellie could think, or speak, or try to run away, Catherine lifted a shaking arm.

"You," she breathed. "You murderer. *You* killed him, and as good as killed Maid Marian! And *you*." She turned on the rest of the League. "Turner was right about you, you traitors!"

Jacob saw what she was about to do and lunged to stop her, but it was too late: She stuck her head out the door and began to scream.

"The Galpins are harboring a murderer! Elinor Dray! The girl who killed Robin Hood!"

"Ellie, get out of here," Jacob cried. "Out the back door, *go*!"

She ran into the next room. But when she flung the door open, a curious few were already approaching.

"That's her!" shouted Andrew Newgate. "The Dray girl!"

As his cries drew more people toward the house, Ellie slammed the door shut and rushed back into the front room. Margery and Jacob had managed to push Catherine out the door but couldn't get it closed behind her.

"She's in there!" Catherine shrieked. "Elinor Dray!" The door flew open, sending Margery and Jacob staggering into the wall. Catherine and both the Ward boys pushed their way in, and Ellie could hear the cries of more people coming. Andrew Newgate ran in from the kitchen, a sour-faced Lucy Mason at his heels.

The fight was at such close range, their bows did no good. Margery was swinging hers like a scythe, and Alice was screaming and kicking her feet as Andrew Newgate lifted her up and passed her over his head to Thomas Mason, who carried her out the front door. Ralf and Jacob punched out doggedly and kicked whoever they could reach, but it wasn't enough.

Ellie thought she saw an opening between Catherine Baker and one of the Ward boys, barely older than her and holding a horseshoe in one hand. She was ready to dive for it, when a hot, sickly flash of pain made her vision echo itself. She staggered to the side, and then the cool of the floor was under her back.

The crowd surged above her. For a fearful minute she thought she'd be trampled before anyone could pick her up. Suddenly Tom Turner's vicious face was over hers, too close.

"Got you this time, Dray," he sneered. His foot was on her bow, pressing against the bend of it. For a terrified moment Ellie thought it might snap. But with a grin Turner stood back. "On your feet, girl. You'll hang before the sun goes down."

He grabbed her roughly by the shoulders and stood her up, facing the door. Vaguely she saw her four friends just outside, their hands tied with lengths of rope. A bruise was blooming on Margery's cheek, and the sight made Ellie burn with fury. As Tom Turner leered over her, she took a breath and drove her head straight into his nose. He screamed and reeled backward, clutching his face. Blood spurted through his fingers.

Ellie saw her chance. She ran straight for Ralf and began plucking at the rope around his hands. It was so tight his skin was already starting to scrape away.

"No time," Ralf said urgently. "Get out of here, Ellie!"

"I'm not leaving you!" She pawed desperately at the knots.

Ralph swung around, shoving her away with his shoulder. His face was as serious as the grave. "They'll hang you if you stay. Go! Run!"

And Ellie did. She dashed around the house and into the yard, where she paused to stare blindly around her. Too frantic to think, she just needed a place to hide. *The chicken coop? The stable?*

Finally she did what she'd always done when she needed to escape: She ran to the woods. Hearing shouts behind her, she stopped at an oak just past the forest's edge and began to climb. She'd passed into its leafy crown when a few villagers crashed past her, far below. They didn't think she'd have the nerve to hide so close.

But she was too shattered by what had happened to feel even the smallest flush of victory. Even though she knew Ralf was right, and she'd no doubt have a noose about her neck if she'd stayed a moment longer, she felt sick with shame. She pressed her face into her hands. The League had given up everything for her, and here she was, alive and unhurt, while they were Tom Turner's prisoners. What if she never saw them again? How would she manage without Ralf, without any of them?

Huddled in the treetop, she wept. When she finally looked up, she saw between the leaves the perfect, flat blue sky of evening. She was all alone. Without the League she was done for. And by the time the sun rose the next morning, Maid Marian would be dead.

# 21

ELLIE CROUCHED AMONG THE TANGLED ROOTS of the Greenwood Tree. As the afternoon waned, she'd climbed back down the oak tree and found her way to Robin Hood's hideout. Tuck was gone, the League in the hands of the villagers. She was all alone with the ghosts of the Merry Men.

The tree's trunk was solid against her back, but it wasn't enough to soothe her. Her mind spun around and around, like a sick dog trying to settle. *They won't hurt them,* she thought, seeing her friends with their hands tied. *They'll just scare them, then send them home to their parents.*

But she'd seen the bloodlust in Tom Turner's eyes. If he had his way, they'd all pay for her "crime"—the Galpins, too.

Without her friends and the sanctuary of the abbey, forever a fugitive of the baron's cruel justice, she could have no kind of life. Even her childish dreams of living here in the forest with Friar Tuck flickered and died like a candle.

Ellie breathed in the phantom scent of old campfires, could almost hear the music of long-ago voices—Robin's, Maid Marian's. Then she climbed to her feet. No more bedtime stories. All she could do now was try to make good on the one promise she still could: to save Maid Marian.

She needed to get those keys back. When she'd walked by Tom Turner's house with the bowl under her dress, she'd wondered: *Did he keep the keys himself? Turn them in, toss them in a ditch?* But she was willing to bet on his selfishness. He wouldn't give up his prize, even if he had no use for it.

From the forest's edge the path to Turner's house was short but perilous. Ellie moved along the backs of houses, tiptoeing around Helen Pygott's irritable flock of clucking hens, and ducking when she passed the window where Lucy Mason leaned to take in the air, singing an off-key ballad. She threw herself down in the dirt when a whistling Ellen Ward passed too close.

Finally she reached Turner's. With silent fingers she let herself in through his front door.

The stench of liquor and unclean skin hit her like a mallet. The house was one filthy room, nearly empty in the firelight. A grimy bedroll was pushed against the wall, far too close to a huge bucket filled with rotting apples and attended by flies. Turner sold just enough of his apple liquor to feed himself, and drank the rest. The house was nicer once, she remembered. When his wife and son still lived there, before his drinking drove them away.

With the door closed, the heat from Turner's flickering fire was oppressive. It offered barely enough light to see by—so it took her at least a minute to realize she wasn't alone. Turner lay half propped against the wall, hugging his tankard to his chest with one arm.

Ellie froze, a rabbit in the shadow of a circling hawk—but then he began snoring loudly. Still, she counted his labored breaths, reaching ten before she let herself move again.

She started with the bedroll, pillaging through the greasy sheets and patting the pillow, finally daring to flip the whole thing over. Nothing. She ran her hands along the underside of a crude wooden table, taking a hissing breath as a splinter embedded itself in her palm. She shook out piles of grimy cloth and searched the inside of Turner's hunting bag. At every moment she expected a snort, followed by a shout, as he woke up to find she'd walked right into his den.

When Ellie had checked over the house inch by inch, she still hadn't found anything—not the keys, not the arrow, not the gold. If she'd had to guess, she'd have said the money at least was nestled somewhere on his person, waiting to be traded for pints at the nearest tavern.

But the keys . . . Ellie's eye fell on the bucket. With mingled hope and dread she kneeled in front of it. Then, turning her head away and folding her lips shut tight, she plunged one arm into the muck.

When she reached bottom, her arm was submerged nearly to the shoulder, and her eyes were running from the fumes. An angry fly buzzed against her cheek as she scrabbled her fingers through the fermenting fruit.

Then they caught against something hard and slender in all that slop. *The arrow.* She gasped and caught it up, and felt around until she had the keys, too. She stood quickly, trying to shake the wretchedness from her arm, then wrapped her finds in her cloak.

Head down, she crept past Turner, who muttered something in his sleep.

Then his arm shot out and grabbed hers.

"Thief," he slurred, twisting her wrist. Then, louder, "Thief!"

*He doesn't know who I am*, Ellie realized. If he knew whom he'd caught, he'd call for help. He'd do anything not to lose her again.

His tankard still hung loosely from his other hand. She snatched it and swung it hard, catching him square against the side of the head. His eyes opened, stunned, and then slipped half-shut as he fell backward—his fingers letting go of her wrist.

Clutching the arrow and keys, she took off toward the door, letting the tankard clatter to the floor as she flung it open and ran.

It was getting late. The woods faded from hazy blue to purple as she ran under the trees. She had Robin's bow and his silver arrow. She had the baron's keys. And she had the abbess's face in her mind, warm and wise.

But that was all she had. If she got caught now, she'd lose the time she needed to save Maid Marian. Without friends to help her escape, she'd have nothing to look forward to but the noose. What was it Mother Barkbone had called Robin Hood? *The hooded man.* She understood it now. You had to hide your face to live the outlaw's life. Not just to save your own skin, but to hide from those you'd wronged, for good or ill.

The baron's castle rose slowly over the treetops as she approached it from the north. In the gathering darkness, it looked more imposing than ever, a vast and impenetrable pile of ancient stone. Ellie crept from tree to tree, then bush to bush, until she was as close as she dared to its drawbridge. It was open but guarded by two fierce-looking men in dull chain mail and helmets. Each had a bow over his shoulder and a sword at his waist.

A cart rattled past Ellie, slowing to a halt just before the bridge. Its driver, a thin, gray-haired man, hunched over the reins.

"Boots on the ground!" barked one of the baron's men. The driver hesitated, and the guard repeated himself, voice rising. Finally the man climbed down, his age showing in his careful movements. The first guard waited with a drawn sword while the other hopped onto the cart. He moved through its piles of supplies, kicking at laden sacks and stabbing his sword into the straw.

Finally he nodded and jumped down. "Now turn out your pockets, and off with the cap," he said, while the first guard bent down to check the underside of the cart. When he straightened up, Ellie could make out the cold smile beneath the lip of his helmet. "And something for our trouble," he said, putting out a hand.

"But . . . I . . . ," the old man stammered.

"Come on, grandfather. You want us telling the baron

you were bringing something in—a bow and arrows for the prisoner, perhaps?"

As the old man patted his pockets for a coin, Ellie's disgust at the guards was cut with a thin triumph. The baron had Maid Marian under lock and key, and order of death, but still he couldn't rest easy. All these extra measures . . . he was *expecting* someone to try to save her.

Once the cart passed, nothing else happened for a long time. The guards stared straight ahead, not even joking between themselves. The sky turned black and the moon climbed high over the keep. And still Ellie crouched, deep in thought.

Even if she could slip past them, she'd be seen on the bridge before she got any distance. The walls were thick, the gray stone too uniform to climb. It was a sheer, breathless drop into the dark waters of the moat. If she could make it there, she was a strong enough swimmer to reach the back of the castle—but there'd be no way to climb the slippery wall once she got there. And each window in the castle was an eye out of which someone might peek—the baron, one of his servants or guards. She couldn't risk being seen.

After almost an hour of frustrated thought, she'd gotten nowhere. Outlawry, she reflected, wasn't something you could do on your own. *I need the League.*

She was almost ready to give in, to just dunk herself in the moat and hope a second half of the plan would fall into place on its own, when something moved in the bushes on the other side of the road, just beyond the guards' line of sight.

Not a breeze, and not a rabbit. Holding as still as she could, she let the darkness slowly resolve into something: a gray hood. Someone was there, someone who'd just given away his or her hiding place.

For a long moment she watched, hoping the person might make a move—stand up and address the guards, or run at them with a hidden sword. *Friend or foe?* she thought. Even if this person was against the baron, it didn't necessarily mean the person was on her side.

She'd have to find out for herself. Silently Ellie stood, wincing as her muscles came back to life. Quiet as a cat, she crossed the road and crept up behind the hooded figure. As she drew an arrow out of its quiver, the person seemed to sense something and started to turn. Ellie quickly pressed her arrow into the back of the person's neck.

"On your knees."

The person froze, then lowered slowly into a crouch. A man, she could see now, lifting rough hands into a gesture of submission.

"Who are you?" she whispered. "And what do you want?"

"May I turn?" he replied. His voice was steadier than she thought it would be. Ellie stepped back, just far enough for him to turn toward her on his knees.

She twitched with recognition when she saw his face. Deeply tanned skin, close-cropped beard, and eyes that might be blue in better light. Those eyes widened when he saw the person threatening him was a twelve-year-old girl.

"Hello," he said, his hands starting to drop. In a flash Ellie had drawn her bow, placing an arrow in it. He lifted his hands back up to the sky.

"Who are you?"

"A disloyal subject to the king," he deadpanned. "And you?"

His voice was familiar—and then it hit her. He was at the tavern where she'd met Tuck, one half of the fight over Robin and the Merry Men that the friar had broken up.

"I heard you," she blurted out. "In the Swan. Defending Robin."

He seemed thrown for a moment by the change of subject, then nodded slowly. "I won't ask what you were doing in a tavern," he said. "But yes, I remember that night."

She was wasting precious time, she knew. But after everything she'd learned about Robin, she needed to know. "What makes you so loyal to him still?" she asked. "Do you really think, after all he's done—all the people he's killed—that he deserves your defense?"

"Ah." The man's light-colored eyes roamed over her face. "I think I know who you are. Elinor something, isn't it? The girl blamed for his death."

Her stone silence was enough for him. He nodded and let his arms drop, just a fraction. "I wasn't defending just Robin Hood," he said, "but the Merry Men as well. It's true Robin did some terrible things in his life, and perhaps his time had come. We all must pay up for our deeds on earth eventually. But he did good, too, you must remember. I couldn't say which outweighs the other."

Now his hands were down, pressed against his thighs as he kneeled, looking up at Ellie.

"You knew him, didn't you?" she said. "I can hear it in your voice."

The man dipped his head in assent. "More than knew him. Robin was like a brother to me."

"And you are?"

"I'm Will Scarlet."

## 22

THE MAN SAID HIS NAME WEARILY, LIKE HE'D tired of it. Or of what it meant to bear it.

Ellie gasped. *If only Ralf were here*, she thought wistfully. Will Scarlet had been not just the youngest and most dashing of the Merry Men, but the most skilled at swordplay. Ellie remembered hearing a minstrel sing of him once in Nottingham, of his good looks and the red silk tunic he wore to match his name.

He wasn't wearing it now. She could still see the traces of the young dandy in his eyes, but his clothing was old and his skin was as tanned as boot leather.

"You're here to save Marian, aren't you?" she asked avidly. "And they're coming to meet you—the Merry Men?"

He made a sound between a laugh and a snort. "I'm here for Marian, yes. But I'm on my own. Robin's men have scattered like thistle seeds these past five years. Some too far to hear of his death, some too drunk to care. Some dead themselves. And some—some may be close but unwilling to forgive Robin."

His eyes darkened as he spoke, and Ellie didn't dare ask what he meant. She felt a kinship with this man, hunkered in the darkness at the side of the baron's road. Lost to his friends, conflicted about the man who had once been a brother to him—just as Ellie didn't know how to feel about the same man, who once was her hero.

"I'm alone too," she said slowly. "If we work together, we'll have a real chance at saving her."

Will Scarlet was shaking his head even before she stopped speaking. "I've been watching the castle from every side. It would take more than an old man and a little girl to pull this off."

Ellie shook off his slight and took out her hard-won ring of keys. "But I have these."

His eyebrows rose in silent surprise. "They'd get us in," he began, then shook his head again. "But how will we get out? Alive, and with Marian unharmed? It's useless."

Frustration rose up in Ellie, threatening to choke her. "So we just let her die? What kind of outlaw are you?"

"The kind that has managed to outlive every one of his friends." The words weren't bitter or boastful, but resigned.

"I thought Marian was your friend," Ellie said quietly.

Will Scarlet stood, his tall shape blocking out the moon behind him. "And it looks like I'll outlive her, too."

There was so much sorrow in his face, Ellie felt sad instead of angry. Then she remembered something she'd forgotten about in the wild rush of the day. "Robin's funeral," she whispered.

"What's that?"

"Robin's funeral, at your old encampment—not the Greenwood Tree, but the other place. Friar Tuck told me about it. I thought I would go, but . . ." But she wasn't sure she could pay her respects to Robin Hood. She wasn't sure he really deserved them. "But I still haven't cleared my name," she finished. "Anyone there to honor Robin will probably think killing me would be the best way to do it."

Will Scarlet rested a rough hand on her shoulder—just for a moment. "Some will believe you, girl. It sounds like Friar Tuck did. Perhaps I'll go myself."

"Do you believe the Merry Men will come?"

"Robin will be there," he said simply. "It's important to make your peace with the dead, even if—especially if—you've wronged each other in life. Perhaps I'll see you there. If not, I wish you luck. And peace. If I know Maid Marian, it's what she would want. For all of her friends." Then he hesitated, looking for a long moment at her face. "My son would be about your age. I'd be proud if he were like you. You have honor. I think Robin would've liked you too."

Then he was gone, striding toward the woods. Ellie didn't dare call out to him with the guards so close. Long after he'd disappeared, she still stared in the direction he'd gone.

Then she crept back along the road to take a last look at the castle. The guards stared out into the dark, the impenetrable keep hunched behind them. Somewhere inside it the abbess was saying her final prayers—or holding out hope for a rescue that would never come.

Will Scarlet was right: Saving Marian was impossible. The only thing Ellie could do now was pay her last respects to Robin, for the sake of the woman they both loved. Blinking back tears, she walked into the woods. Her heart grew heavier with every step that took her farther from Marian.

She'd been walking for less than an hour when she nearly stumbled into the path of someone moving purposefully through the woods. She darted behind a tree and watched the person pass.

It was a woman, hooded and holding a candle in cupped hands. It felt like a miracle that the tiny flame stayed lit. Ellie resumed her trek, but soon a man, woman, and child walked by not twenty paces from where she stood. Each held a candle and paid her no mind. The closer she came to Robin's burial ground, the place where his silver arrow had fallen, the more people she saw in the trees. She pulled her hood up but felt no fear. Everyone carried a candle, their faces solemn in the glow.

All that couldn't prepare her for what she saw when she reached the clearing. A sea of people, all hooded and holding their small, warm lights. An old man leaning against a cart full of candles pressed one into her palm, and a girl barely older than Ellie used her own to light it. With a start Ellie realized she was one of the Ward girls, her face soft in the orange glow. Ellie bobbed her head in thanks, then shrank away before the girl could recognize her.

*Are these all true mourners?* she wondered. *Or are some the baron's spies?* Many were strangers, but she saw Andrew and Ellen Newgate, and Allan Payne surrounded by his sons and their wives. Lucy Mason was there, her arm linked with that of a man Ellie didn't recognize. Then Friar Tuck stepped into the center of the murmuring crowd, his face aglow.

He raised his arms and the crowd hushed, settling into a ring around the towering friar. "You've gathered here despite the danger," he began, his voice thick with emotion. "Under the baron's nose, in the very woods he claims as his own, you've come to pay your respects to the Crown's greatest enemy and the poor man's greatest friend. There is no better homage you can pay to Robin Hood than to be here tonight." Tuck bowed his head. Latin prayers, melodic and haunting, unwound from his tongue and settled into Ellie's bones. Under a sky smudged with stars, surrounded by pinpricks of candlelight and rows of quiet faces, Ellie felt her misgivings about Robin Hood move to the back of her mind. For this moment, at least, she thought only of the man who'd saved her village. Who'd given the people hope. Who'd shot two ducks in the dark one night, and spoken of carrying the weight of the world on his back.

When the ceremony was over, Friar Tuck paused a long moment, his tonsured head bowed in prayer, then addressed the crowd in English. "Thank you for coming so far tonight. I regret that I couldn't perform this service in a more convenient location." There was the edge of a smile on his mouth. "You're all welcome here. Any who wish to pay homage to Robin Hood may speak."

A brief pause, then an old man stepped forward.

**LEAGUE OF ARCHERS**

"It's thanks to Robin my daughter is alive," he said tremulously, looking back at a smiling woman behind him. Ellie recognized her as Mary Carpenter, whose son, Gregory, was lying in the abbey hospital. Her heart ached to think that he wasn't here to see this.

"When she got sick, we could afford no medicine," the old man continued. "The doctor refused to help us if we couldn't pay. I don't know how he heard about our plight, but Robin sent a healer to our doors. She saved . . . *he* saved my daughter's life."

His cheeks shone with tears as he stepped back. Someone else stepped forward to tell his own story of gratitude. Then another, and another. It felt like every person there had something to say about their hero— even if the stories didn't all have perfect endings, or even happy ones.

"We were next to starving one winter when Robin brought us a fat calf," Andrew Newgate said ruefully. "The thing is, he stole it from a rich man just one town over, and that man traced it back to me. He caught me at my supper table, mouth wet with calf fat. I spent two days in the stocks for it!" There was a pause, then he shouted with laughter, and the crowd followed. Even Ellie had to laugh at the picture of Newgate tucking into his stolen dinner, right in front of the one it had been stolen from.

Now the tenor of the stories changed as people shared funny memories about Robin. Helen Pygott blushed as she told of the night he stole her heart at a summer dance, then walked off with a pig from her father's sty. Another spoke of watching Robin cheat his way through another man's purse over a gambling table—then disappear when the other man went to relieve himself.

Like everyone else, Ellie couldn't stop smiling. But the stories touched something inside her too. This was the Robin Hood she'd grown up believing in—a man who made people's lives better—before she started to question the cost. She remembered what she had said to the League the night Robin died. It felt like a hundred lifetimes ago. "It's not the man that's important," she'd said, "it's what he stands for." And the idea of Robin Hood was one she could hold close to her heart forever.

Finally the stories tapered off, and someone pulled out a lute and played a mournful tune. People mingled, speaking quietly, and Ellie wandered through the crowd. She bumped into a short, hooded figure and turned to grunt an apology—then stopped short.

"Alice!" she said.

Alice looked up in surprise, letting her hood fall back. "Ellie?"

Ellie saw the rest of the League gathered around her.

"You're here," she said, almost crying with relief. "You're not in prison!"

"They let us go," Jacob said. "They aren't bad people. Just confused, and worked up by that foolish Tom Turner."

Ralf was still staring at her. "You're safe," he said. Then he wrapped her in a tight hug.

"Because of you," she said, pulling away. She grinned at her friends, drinking in their faces, barely able to believe they were here. "I wouldn't have survived this long without you. I'm lost without the League."

"Just like Robin was lost without his Merry Men," Ralf said. He gestured at the crowd. "He wasn't perfect, was he? But he was *good*."

"No outlaw can be perfect," Ellie replied fervently. "But as long as England is ruled by men like King John and Lord de Lays, we'll need outlaws. Outlaws like Robin Hood."

"Hear, hear," said Ralf, lifting his candle like a glass. "We'll have to find a new one now, I guess. Someone who can fight like he could."

"And make guards quiver like little girls," Jacob added. Alice threw him a look, and he rolled his eyes. "Like oak leaves, I mean. Quiver like oak leaves."

"And they'll need to be willing to steal," Margery added, "but never keep a penny of it for themselves."

"Will Scarlet!" Ellie said suddenly. Her friends looked at her, surprised, and she rushed to explain. "I met him tonight—he was trying to save Marian too."

Ralf gaped at her. "Will Scarlet! What was he like? Did he have his sword with him? Did he—"

Ellie interrupted him with a laugh. "He said he'd be here. If we find him, you can see for yourself!"

They moved through the crowd, searching.

"He's tall and blue eyed," Ellie said. "Younger than Tuck, though his face is rough."

But locating him proved an impossible task. If Will Scarlett had been there, he'd already melted back into the trees. Ralf looked glum.

"He turned up once," Ellie told him. "Maybe he'll turn up again."

The stars were still bright in the sky, but the darkness was lifting. The hazy glow of dawn was starting to appear— the last dawn Marian would see, unless the League did something.

"I didn't know how to save Marian by myself," Ellie said. "I gave up. But the five of us . . . I think we have a chance. Will you come with me to the baron's castle?"

"Of course," Ralf said without hesitation as they all nodded. "We're in."

A man in a cloak towered over them, his face lost in

shadows. "Did I hear you say you're going to rescue Maid Marian?"

Ellie felt Ralf tense at her side, hand on his knife. She hesitated and then squared her shoulders. "Yes. We are."

"But how? How can that possibly be done?" More people gathered behind him, drawn by his loud voice.

"It can't be," a woman scoffed. "They're children. There's nothing they know that we don't."

*But there is*, Ellie thought, longing to throw back her hood and reveal all. Then she paused. Why couldn't she do just that? There was no better way to grab their attention than to reveal herself as the infamous Elinor Dray.

Quickly she located the friar in the crowd.

"Tuck," she said, grabbing his hand. "I'm about to do something stupid. Will you back me up?"

He took her in and then nodded. "Of course, child. Here."

She took the candle he pressed into her hand, and stepped carefully onto a tree stump near the edge of the clearing. Then she took a deep breath and threw back her hood.

"My name is Elinor Dray!"

Her voice was loud against the hush. All around her, eyes widened in surprised recognition, then narrowed.

"It's the girl who killed Robin Hood!" a woman spat.

"How dare you show up here," a man growled, pushing toward her. "This is a sacred place."

"Stand down!" Friar Tuck bellowed, his voice so full of righteous fury the man froze in the act of grabbing Ellie by the tunic. "Give her space, and let her speak."

The people nearest Ellie backed up, until she was ringed in a circle of suspicious faces. Margery nodded at her encouragingly, and Ellie opened her mouth.

"Maid Marian will be executed at dawn," she began.

"That's no secret," a woman grumbled, then fell silent at a glare from Tuck.

"We've no time to argue over who killed Robin Hood," Ellie insisted. "Not if we want to have any chance of rescuing her."

A few men stepped forward, as if to disagree, and she saw her words wouldn't be enough.

"But I can tell you I'm innocent. And that I believe the baron is behind it. You can ask Mother Barkbone, who made the poison that killed Robin. Or George Galpin, who made the arrow. Both will tell you they sold their wares to grown men. And Friar Tuck himself believes me when I say it: I did not kill Robin Hood. I was framed by the baron—because he did it."

She pulled the keys from where she'd tucked them in her tunic and held them aloft. "I have the means to get

Marian out of her cell. But I'll need help getting her out of the castle after that. Will you help me? Will you help Marian?"

Silence followed her words. The people pressing in around her looked at one another, as if deciding whether to believe her based on the opinions of their neighbors.

"I'll stand with you, Elinor Dray," the friar rumbled. "I'm a man of God, one of Robin's greatest friends. And I believe your only crime was trying to help Robin—and getting in the baron's way."

"I'll stand with you too," said the tall man who'd first heard them talking. "I can't let such a noble woman hang."

More voices shouted out in agreement, and more supporters joined Ellie's growing band. Many more melted away into the forest, either unconvinced or too fearful to join the cause, but finally about twenty remained.

Seeing their determined faces gathered in the moonlight, a mix of villagers, strangers, and her oldest friends, Ellie felt as if her heart might burst. Maybe—just maybe—it was enough to save Marian.

# 23

IT WAS AN HOUR BEFORE DAWN, AND NERVES
had sizzled all of Ellie's tiredness away. She stood with
Tuck and her ragged band of supporters at the edge of the
woods, looking up at the crouching shadow of the baron's
castle. Some of them seemed less certain now, but enough
stood strong, jaws set and eyes glaring toward the place
Maid Marian was meant to hang. Everyone was shadowy
shapes in the dark—they didn't dare light a torch so close
to the baron's gates.

Ellie felt the friar's hand, heavy on her elbow. "Please
reconsider," he said to her and the rest of the League. "You're
young, with your lives stretching before you. I've lived mine
already—we can make a new plan. Let this be my fight."

"It's been mine since the baron took my mother abbess away." She looked around at her friends, the guilt she'd tried to push down breaking free of its gates. "But you don't have to go with me," she told them. "We have more people now—it's not hopeless. Your parents are still alive, and I don't know what they'd do without you. . . ."

"Ellie," Ralf said firmly. "We're going with you."

"We're good in a fight," Jacob told the friar.

"And some of us are small and sneaky," Alice added.

Tuck nodded in defeat, then went over the plan once more. Finally they split into two groups: The friar and the other adults set off down the castle road, and the League crept swiftly along the overgrown ground beside it. When they reached the castle, they pressed themselves tight along the wall in the shadows beneath the open drawbridge.

Ellie watched in awe as Friar Tuck marched straight toward the guards, the other rescuers in tow.

The guards drew their swords. "Stop there, old man!" one of them yelled. The friar kept walking, his hood pulled close to his tonsured head. Then he opened his mouth and started to sing.

*"Said Queen Jane to the minstrel, sing a song in my ear*
*Fiddle fee, fiddle fi, fiddle rum pum, pum, pum,*

*For the king has no talent on the pipes nor the lyre*

*Fiddle fee, fiddle fi, fiddle rum pum, pum, pum."*

"Is it working? I can't see if it's working!" Ralf whispered.

"Shh!" Ellie elbowed him, watching in astonishment as the friar swaggered forward, still singing his bawdy song. The guards tensed, hands on their swords, then froze in confusion as Tuck swept forward and drew one, then both, into a hug.

"Happy Christmas!" he yelled. The rest of the crowd took up his cry, shaking hands with the confused guards and slapping them on the back.

"Now see here," one of them started, "stop that tomfoolery! It's not Christmas for months." But a pretty, light-haired woman pressed a jug of ale into his hand. He shrugged, then took a swig.

"Now!" Ellie said.

The guards were surrounded and didn't see the League slip out of their hiding place, then file silently past. They stayed in the thick shadows along one side of the bridge, tiptoeing at first, then breaking out into a run. Soon the sound of false revelry behind them faded, replaced by the faint lapping of the moat against the castle walls.

Finally the courtyard yawned before them. A boy

carrying a saddle slung over one shoulder ran toward them, and they stepped sharply back into the shadows. Ellie held her breath till he was past, then nodded and led the League into the dark. Lit sconces hung beside the massive doors, casting flickering shadows over the yard and the carvings around the entrance, stone faces that could have belonged to griffins or kings. Ellie cut left, praying there was another way in. When she spied a small guard door, she breathed out with relief. She bent over it, holding her ring of keys—but with a horrible clatter they fell from her sweaty palms.

For a moment the whole League froze. Ellie looked up at the slitted windows overhead, waiting for the cry, the singing arrow, but all was silent. She snatched up the keys and got to work fitting the right one into the lock. Finally one slipped in with an easy *thunk* as sweet as birdsong, and she eased open the door to the castle.

As they stepped, blinking, into a narrow corridor, the smoke of a dozen lamps lining the walls made the air thick.

"We can't go in armed," she whispered. "They'll seize us as soon as they see our weapons." She let Robin's bow fall to the floor, then wedged it into a corner and covered it with rushes. She ignored the nagging fear that she'd never see it again. The rest of the League followed suit.

"Now grab anything you can find," Ellie said, "and act like it's your job to carry it. If you look like you're meant to be here, no one will think you aren't."

It was a thin plan but the best they had. Jacob wrenched two lamps off the walls, the candles flickering inside them, and handed them to Alice and Ellie. Then he straightened up and walked superciliously behind them, carrying his staff—his clothes were the nicest, he could get away with it. Margery spied a tarnished tray half-buried in the rushes, and Ralf made do with a stinking armful of the rushes themselves.

Then they reached the end of the corridor and were suddenly in the bustle of the hall. Though it was nearly dawn, the room was a hive of activity: servants moving every which way, Frenchmen in their cloaks, a young man strumming a stringed instrument, dogs tussling over bones thrown into the rushes. The long tables were scattered with platters and drained cups of wine. Laughter carried over the music, and a few men snoozed in their chairs, heads laid back or in their plates; the room had the air of a festival on its last legs. They'd been celebrating, Ellie realized. The death of Maid Marian was being treated like a holiday. *They won't get their hanging*, Ellie swore to herself.

Then she saw the baron, slouched drunkenly on his throne. Her heart gave a sickly thump. She'd nearly missed him—he was so wrapped in ridiculous finery, he looked more like a stack of velvets than a man. But when the fiddler put down his bow to wipe his forehead, the baron roused himself. "Play on," he said sharply.

The music started again. "What do we do?" asked Margery in a panicked whisper. But the baron was already letting his head loll back, the cup in his hand tipping perilously. Carefully the League moved around the room in a loose cluster, trying to look as though they belonged. In order to find the dungeons, they'd have to go below the castle—it was just a matter of finding the right door.

Then, rising before them like a bogeyman in a bad dream, there was Gilbert, the servant Ellie had robbed on the road. His hair looked greasier than ever, and he was strutting importantly through the room with a pitcher of wine.

Ellie spun around to face the wall, expecting to be seized at any moment. When a hand grabbed her shoulder, she thought desperately of her bow lying tucked in the straw.

Gilbert stood over her, stinking of kitchen and sour grapes. "What are you doing here?"

Ellie forced herself not to look at her friends, but she could see them from the corner of her eye. Ralf looked half-ready to launch himself onto Gilbert. "I . . . I was just—" she began.

"Go! To the kitchen, and bring back another barrel. The baron doesn't pay your keep so you'll stand here gawking."

He gave her ear a hard twist and turned away. It took a moment for Ellie to catch her breath, and she jumped when Ralf put a hand on her arm. "We can't hide in here much longer," she said urgently.

Just then she saw a man holding a tray bearing a hunk of bread and a small measure of oily-looking wine. She noted the key ring at his waist, and her breath quickened.

"Gareth!"

The man holding the tray turned at the sound of the baron's voice, and Ellie ducked her head, leading the League into a part of the hall that the firelight didn't reach. A man snored against the wall, and a dog tried to eat the chicken leg clutched in his fingers.

"That's the prisoner's final meal, is it?" The baron's voice was laced with malice.

"Yes, sir." The servant called Gareth approached the throne, brandishing his tray. "Bread and wine, what we usually give the prisoners."

The baron sent the tray clattering into the straw. "She's no ordinary prisoner," he hissed. "Give her the bones. The ones the dogs won't touch. She'll not get another morsel from me."

Gareth hesitated, then bent to gather his tray and a few bones from the rushes. He straightened up, then left through a door behind the baron's throne.

The League waited until the baron's head lolled back again, his hand playing out the fiddler's lively tune on the air. Then they walked as calmly as they could, following in Gareth's footsteps. His back was just disappearing at the end of a smoke-blackened hall. The passageway was narrow and stopped suddenly at a perilously steep stone staircase, which wound down in a spiral as tight as Margery's curls. Far below, Ellie could see Gareth's lamp bobbing as he descended. When the light was out of view, she and her friends followed.

Ellie didn't dare bring the lamp with her into the dark and gestured at Margery to leave hers at the top of the stairs. The League held on to one another's tunics with one hand, using the other to feel along the wall. While the hall was warm with firelight, lamps here were scarce, burning coldly against the dark.

Finally they reached the dirt floor and cellar air of the dungeons. When Gareth came suddenly back into view, his hands now empty of the tray, they ducked into an open cell.

Ellie imagined Gareth turning his head, smiling evilly as he realized they'd trapped themselves, and locking the door behind them. But he moved past without incident. When his footsteps had faded away overhead, they rushed from the cell.

Nobody spoke. Even Jacob didn't have a ready joke. They walked under archways of cold brick, their footsteps dulled by scattered straw. The place would feel almost like a chapel, Ellie thought, if it weren't for the stench.

And the rats. They rustled in the corners, their eyes flashing red in the flickering shreds of lamplight. *Could Maid Marian really be here?* Ellie wondered. She was both appalled at the idea of finding Marian in this horrible place and terrified she wouldn't be there. It was nearly dawn. What if she'd been taken to the gallows already?

Then Ellie saw her, sitting on the floor of a cell, her back against damp stone slimy with mold. The abbey's jeweled Bible was open in her lap, and her lips moved silently as she read from it. Ellie was glad that the baron had at least been merciful enough to allow Marian her precious Bible when she needed its comfort the most. And even gladder that Mary Ursula hadn't been poring over it in her absence.

At the sound of the League's approach, Marian lifted her head proudly. When she saw Ellie, her eyes widened. In the next moment she was on her feet, reaching her hands through the grate covering her cell.

"You've found me, Elinor," she said hoarsely.

Ellie gripped Marian's hands, telling herself fiercely not to cry. The abbess was terribly thin and dressed in sackcloth, but her stature was straight and proud. And her eyes were dry.

"I'm so proud of you, and so grateful. To all of you," she said, looking past Ellie at the League. "But we must hurry—the guard told me to say my final prayers. We have little time!"

With numb fingers and a desperate heart, Ellie fumbled her way to the proper key. When she found it, the sound of the lock turning made Marian close her eyes and clasp her hands in brief prayer. She tucked the Bible into a pocket of her cloak.

They went back the way they had come, even more cautiously now that Marian was with them. When they reached the top of the staircase, their lamps were still there, which Ellie took as a good sign.

"How are we supposed to get her through that awful party?" Ralf whispered. But when Ellie peeked out into the hall, it was nearly empty. The minstrel had fallen asleep at the foot of the baron's throne, and a Frenchman lay snoring across one table, wrapped in his purple cloak. Exhausted servants took no notice of him as they cleared the tables, and they certainly took no notice of the League.

"They all must have left for the gallows." Marian pointed out the window to where a rim of daylight clung to the tops of the castle walls. "We have to hurry—they'll be coming to get me soon."

They rushed through the hall. Back in the corridor the League retrieved their weapons, and in moments they were in the castle courtyard, in the bright, fresh air.

Marian breathed like she'd just come up from underwater, staring hungrily at open sky. The vise around Ellie's heart eased a bit, and she dared to believe they might pull this off. If all was going as planned, Friar Tuck had knocked out or otherwise gotten rid of the guards, replacing them with two villagers in borrowed mail for show. "All we have to do is get through the courtyard and over the moat," she whispered to Marian. "Friar Tuck will keep the bridge down and the gates open. If anyone tries to follow us, he'll be ready for my signal."

"Tuck?" Marian whispered, eyes bright. "He's here?"

Ellie grinned and put a finger to her lips. They slunk into the shadows, Marian moving as quietly as any of them. Ellie swelled with excitement, practically feeling the sheltering arms of the woods around her. *We're almost there.*

Then a coarse voice cut her in two. "Hey—you, there! Who's that you've got with you?"

The voice came from the door they'd just left. A guard stood there, his face twisted in the flickering light of his lamp.

"Run!" Ellie said raggedly.

She saw Margery's eyes fill with fear, before she whipped around and started to sprint. Alice was faster than any of them, and Jacob tried to run while drawing his sword at the same time. Marian grabbed up her dress in both hands and followed. "To the devil with these skirts!" she cried.

The man whistled piercingly. "The prisoner is in the courtyard," he yelled. Ellie threw one last look over her shoulder—and saw his eyes go wide with surprise. Then he slumped forward and toppled to the ground.

A man stood behind him holding a club, his face half in shadow.

Marian gasped, gripping Ellie's arm. "My God. Will!"

Ellie had only a moment to feel amazement—and gratitude—that he'd come. In the next, guards flooded into the courtyard from both directions. "Take her alive!" one of them cried. "Take the prisoner alive!"

"Marian!" Will Scarlet pulled a dagger from his boot and threw it, spinning, through the air. Maid Marian caught it by the handle, as neatly as if it were an apple falling from a tree.

No time to gape. Ellie shut her mouth and strung an arrow on her bow. She let it fly into the shoulder of a man looming over Alice with his halberd. He screamed and twisted away, and Jacob knocked his feet out from under him with his staff.

Will Scarlet and Marian fought side by side, moving around each other like dancers. Ellie could almost see the abbess as a girl of sixteen, running away to Sherwood Forest to fight with the Merry Men.

Margery's screech brought her back to herself. Margery had been disarmed by one of the guards; as Ellie watched, Ralf parried him away with his sword, giving Margery time to grab her bow.

"Friar Tuck!" Ellie screamed, forgetting the signal as she grabbed another arrow. "Help us! Now!"

Some of the guards paused in confusion, recognizing the name she'd called. Then the villagers, led by the friar, came thundering down the drawbridge.

Even Ellie was filled with a terrified awe as he ran toward them. He looked as tall as a bear and gripped a sword in each hand. *Now we outnumber the soldiers*, she thought, turning her attention back toward the fight. One of her arrows found the meat of a man's leg as he swung his sword at Marian's exposed side. A second shaved a slice off a guard's ear as he tried to hoist Alice over the side of the drawbridge. When he dropped her, one hand lifting to feel the blood running down his face, she turned on him savagely with her knife.

The courtyard was littered with fallen bodies. Friar Tuck had sheathed one sword and was using his free arm to heave any man who came near him into the dirt. "Get to the bridge!" he yelled. The League and the villagers obeyed, fighting and ducking their way toward it, closer and closer to freedom.

Then a sea of purple cloaks swept through the castle doors: the French soldiers had joined the fight. At their back stood Lord de Lays, a long, slender sword in his hand.

"Bring down the portcullis!" he bellowed.

A guard rushed over to obey his command, and the heavy iron grate that would separate the courtyard from the bridge ground to life. Ellie's heart dropped. If it closed, they'd be trapped inside. She was nearly out of arrows, so she pulled out her hunting knife, ducking under a guard's ax and dashing toward the portcullis. If she could get to it and disarm the man who was closing it, maybe they could still escape with their lives.

But a woman's cry stopped her cold. She spun around to see a guard holding one of the villagers by the hair, making to cut her throat. Ellie paused at the outskirts of the battle and sent one of her arrows flying into his hand.

He let the woman slip, and she scrambled to freedom—then the man pulled out the arrow, tossed it aside, and charged toward Ellie.

He screamed a harsh handful of French words she didn't recognize. So he was one of the baron's Frenchmen, though he wore no purple cloak. The man went after her with a knife held awkwardly in his uninjured left hand. The rush of sheer panic and his fresh injury gave Ellie the advantage, and she was able to knock the knife away before wrenching free of his grasp.

All the French had purple cloaks—but where was his?

She turned blindly toward the guard who was pulling the chain to bring down the portcullis, but he was impossibly distant. The metal teeth at the bottom of it plunged toward the earth, almost there. Once it was down, they would never get out. Her quiver hung light on her shoulder; she grabbed one of her last few arrows.

She'd killed once, to save Friar Tuck, and swore she'd never do it again. But now one man stood between her friends and freedom. In an instant she weighed his death against that of Marian and Will Scarlet, Friar Tuck and the League and herself. And she knew just what Robin would do. Ellie let the arrow fly and watched as it slid into the heart of the guard lowering the gate. The chain fell from his grip, and he dropped to the ground.

"Friar Tuck!" she cried. "Now!"

The friar turned toward the nearly closed portcullis. "Retreat!" he cried. "To the bridge, now!" The villagers not locked in combat, or already fallen, fled toward the bridge. People were crawling desperately under the grate, its spikes pulling at their clothes and ripping their skin. Andrew Newgate threw himself on the chain, straining to open the portcullis high enough for them to escape. She could hardly believe he was the same man who'd tried to capture her that day in the woods. Newgate winced as arrows still flew from the baron's depleted forces; one found Newgate's neck, and he fell back onto the metal grate. Ellie tore her eyes away and picked desperately through the crowd, looking for the League.

"Ellie!" It was Ralf. He and Alice half carried Jacob—bloody faced, nursing a limp—between them.

"Where's Margery?" Ellie screamed.

"I'm here!" She came running toward them, holding her side, one eye circled with a briar of dark bruises.

"You next," Friar Tuck called to them in a voice not worth arguing with. He was guiding Marian under the half-open grate and ushered the League out after her.

When Ellie felt grass beneath her boots again, she nearly dropped with relief.

"Don't wait," Tuck yelled, still ushering their forces off the bridge. "Lose them in the forest!"

They ran as fast as they could, Maid Marian leading the way and Jacob sucking in a breath every time his injured leg took his weight. By the time they reached the trees, Tuck, Will Scarlet, and the rest of the villagers had joined them.

Then Ellie heard the sound of pounding hooves—a phalanx of men on horseback, in mail or purple cloaks, with the baron at their head. She was filled with dark pride: She'd robbed them of their hanging.

"Forget the gallows!" the baron roared. "Kill the wench where she stands!"

"Split up," Ellie panted.

Tuck and the villagers scattered into the trees, but Will grabbed Ellie's arm.

"I know how to lose the baron's men. Keep close behind me."

The light was brighter now, the luminous gray of early dawn right before the sun breaks through. Ellie kept her eyes on Will's narrow back as he led the League first through a thicket that scratched at her face and arms, then over a fallen tree crossing a narrow rift in the earth. Its trunk wobbled as they picked across it, Will turning to watch with somber eyes to see that none of them slipped.

They splashed through a knee-high stream, then crawled under a bare patch of earth under the spreading arms of a fir, ending in a small clearing just twice the size of Ellie's cell in the abbey.

The signs of a recently used camp were there—a burned-out fire, a bedroll. It was Will's, Ellie realized with a start. He had the look of a man who lived outdoors, but that didn't seem right. He'd mentioned his son. And hadn't he been married once, long ago in the golden days of the Merry Men? She was sure she'd heard ballads about it.

Will held a finger to his lips and dropped to a crouch. The rest of them piled into the clearing, then went as still as statues, listening for their pursuers.

First silence, then the slow return of birdsong.

"Safe," Marian breathed. She turned to Ellie and gave her a fierce hug.

"Thank you," she said into Ellie's hair. "For your bravery and my life."

"I just wish I could've discovered who really killed Robin," Ellie said, trying to keep the bitterness from her voice.

"Try to let go of your anger," the abbess said. "You're burdened enough without it."

She turned to Will and hugged him, too.

"I didn't think you'd come. You and Tuck, you're

the only ones. It means the world to me, and would to Robin, too."

Will stiffened, and Marian pulled back, a question in her eyes.

"I just wish . . ." He shook his head. "I just wish my wife and son had been as lucky as you."

Marian touched his hand. "Tuck told me. I'm so sorry for your loss."

He pulled back as if her touch hurt, giving a smile like a wince to soften it. Abruptly he began packing up camp. Ellie watched him shove his few things into the bedroll—a small pot, an extra knife, a shirt. It made her heart ache to see what a life could be reduced to.

"Will, stay." Marian's voice was soft but insistent. "We'll be safer together. We always were."

He made a funny sound, like a laugh with all the joy choked out of it. "I'm a lamed wolf now, Marian, not meant for a pack. Not anymore."

He slung his packed bedroll onto his back, turning his face away. For a moment Ellie thought he might leave it like that, just walk into the woods without saying good-bye. Then he turned and seized both of Marian's hands in his. He kissed them and seemed about to speak. Then he pressed his lips together and stepped back. "Good-bye," he said low, and disappeared into the trees.

His sadness clung to Ellie like smoke. She rubbed the tops of her arms, feeling suddenly cold. "What happened to them? Will's wife and son?"

"They were hanged," Marian said, her eyes on the place where Will had disappeared. "By the Sheriff of Nottingham. He found stolen goods hidden in their cottage—or so he claimed."

Ellie's sadness grew new weight. *If only I'd known,* she thought. There were few people who could really understand the loss of her mother. Will Scarlet was one of them.

Then Ralf gave a strangled cry. Ellie turned to comfort him, and gasped. He was half crouched at the edge of the clearing, holding something in his hand: a rumpled cloak. It was an unmistakable rich purple.

"He forgot this," he said, his face full of naked emotion. "What was Will Scarlet doing with a Frenchman's cloak?"

Then Ellie saw it: a ragged tear in the cloak's hood. Her shock turned into something else, a rush of memories as everything came together into one horrible truth. The guard she'd fought at the baron's castle had worn no cloak—perhaps because it had been stolen. Will was a skilled tracker who knew the woods well enough to disappear into them, leaving behind a trail that seemed to end by magic. He spoke like a local, not a Frenchman.

And the poison—who was to say Mother Barkbone knew what Robin really looked like? A hooded, blue-eyed man buying her poison with gold could give himself any name he chose.

And Robin had done something to him, something bad enough that it caused the Merry Men to disband for good.

Ellie gasped. "It was Will Scarlet," she said breathlessly. "He killed Robin Hood!"

# 24

MAID MARIAN LOOKED AT ELLIE, HER FACE the color of clay. "Come on!" Ellie screamed, then dashed into the woods.

Will Scarlet was the murderer of Robin Hood. His companion. His friend. "Robin was like a brother to me," he'd said. The words scalded Ellie's mind as she sprinted through the trees. How could the brave Will Scarlet have turned so treacherous?

The air was still fresh, but the first heat of day was crawling in. Ellie ran until her feet squelched in her boots and sweat ran into her eyes. She followed broken branches, bent-back greenery. She tracked Will Scarlet like he was a buck she meant to spit with her arrows.

Then she saw, in a sunlit flash, a tree with a symbol carved into it. Two wavering lines; dimly she thought they might mean water was nearby. Then she realized what the carving really signified: She was closing in on the Merry Men's territory. Will Scarlet was heading for the Greenwood Tree.

"He knows these woods better than I do now," Marian said breathlessly, standing beside Ellie. Her voice was full of grief, but running through it was rage, strong as steel.

"We'll find him," Ellie growled. Anger was like embers in her veins, spurring her on. He wouldn't get away with what he'd done. He'd killed Robin, and he'd lied about it. Lied knowing his crime had ruined her life. How many times had she almost died for what Will Scarlet had done? Margery's black eye, Jacob's limp, the new hardness around Alice's eyes and mouth. Maid Marian, thrown in a dank cell and nearly hanged. Ellie's abbey home lost to her forever. All of it was his fault.

Yes, Will Scarlet would pay for what he'd done.

Jacob, on his injured ankle, was lagging behind, and Margery had slowed down to help him. Then Alice pitched face-first over a root, her screech cut off when she landed flat on her stomach. Ralf stopped to help her, but Ellie pushed on.

Even Marian had fallen behind. Ellie was alone now,

only her breath to keep her company, and the rage that filled her like an ache. It dulled the pain of running on an empty stomach and no sleep, in boots worn almost to holes. There was a small clearing ahead; she put on a burst of speed.

"Wait," Marian screamed from behind her. "That's a trap!" Ellie's momentum carried her almost out of the trees, but she managed to grab hold of a sapling. It yanked her back from the edge of another pit trap. The trees on either side of it were carved with a symbol like half a sunburst. *Spikes*, Ellie realized, the hair prickling on her neck. The bottom of the pit must be lined with them.

Then she saw Will, a flash of movement between two distant trees. "Come on!" she said. The League had caught up with her and Marian, and the six of them threaded through the trunks on either side of the pit.

"Watch where I step," said Marian, "and stay close!"

She moved slowly at first, so slowly the frustration of it made Ellie quake. *What if I'm wrong?* she thought. *What if he just keeps going when he reaches the tree?*

But Marian picked up speed as the pattern of traps seemed to come back to her. She pointed out the symbols as she passed them—a crown, the lunar curve of a bow, a handful of slashes that nearly blended into the bark, more of the half starbursts. She stopped short at a hazel tree with a tipped-up shape like a cup carved into it, and peered into its branches.

"Safe now," Marian said. "I don't think Robin reset that one after he ran here from robbing King John himself. . . ." A smile played on her lips. Then she remembered where they were, and it fell away. "Come on."

As they got closer to the Merry Men's hideout, the traps were clustered more thickly. For the first time Ellie truly understood how lucky they'd been, getting in and out safely the first time. *Not luck*, she thought, remembering what Margery had said. The tree had protected them. Perhaps it was protecting them now.

Feeling a renewed urge to reach the tree, to find out the truth, she surged ahead of Marian.

"Ellie, no!"

Ellie turned toward Marian's panicked voice but couldn't stop herself in time. She was stepping through a low cluster of bushes at the base of a rowan tree and felt it when her foot kicked at something that was neither bush nor root. It released the rope she hadn't even seen, rain-worn but intact, snaking up into the rowan's branches.

She tried to scream but couldn't catch her breath, and charged straight ahead because she was too far gone to turn back. A huff of displaced air blew against her neck, followed by a horrible clattering and a crash that sent her diving toward the earth.

When Ellie turned, dusty leaf debris rose from the pile of hewn logs that had rolled out of the tree. Her eyes met Ralf's, standing on the other side. Marian had her arms thrown back, and the League stood behind her, unhurt.

"I suppose we've announced ourselves," Marian said grimly. "If he didn't before, Will knows we're coming now."

Ellie knew she should wait but couldn't bear to stand still while her friends picked their way over the logs. The Greenwood Tree was close now, she could feel it. She trod carefully, watched the trees' trunks for symbols, and finally reached the thick wall of overgrowth that shaded the Merry Men's home from the rest of the forest. Then she stepped through it.

Marian was right: Will Scarlet knew they were coming. He stood waiting for Ellie beneath the Greenwood Tree. He gripped a knife in one hand and crouched in a fighter's stance. Over his head stretched the last sanctuary of the Merry Men; in its roots stood the man who had murdered their leader.

Ellie grabbed the final arrow from her quiver, where it rattled against Robin's silver one. Will did nothing as she nocked it.

"We know you killed him," she said.

A tremor went through him, but his face didn't change.

Ellie let her arrow fly, whistling through the morning and embedding itself into the tree just over his head. Will startled backward, then lost his footing and fell to the ground.

Ellie charged forward, pulling out the silver arrow as she ran. Then she dropped in a crouch just out of the range of his knife and aimed her arrow at his throat. His eyes widened at the sight of it, and he grew still.

"Why did you do it?" It came out in a whisper.

He said nothing, just licked his lips and stared at the glinting silver arrow.

"Do you know what you've done?" she said, her voice shaking. "I nearly died for your crimes. And my friends nearly died trying to clear my name. We're outlaws now because of you. My friends can never go home, never see their families, because you *murdered* Robin Hood. And your last friend, Maid Marian—she almost hanged because of you!"

He cringed at the sound of Marian's name, but still he didn't speak.

"Well?" Ellie said, angling her arrow up so it was pointed at his eye. "Why shouldn't I take my revenge right now?"

"Take your revenge," he gasped finally. "Just as I took mine."

She paused, confused. "What are you saying?"

"See if it makes you happy. See if it brings them back, or keeps their ghosts from visiting you at night." His voice was broken, his eyes haunted.

Ellie fell back on her heels, still keeping the arrow pointed toward his neck. "Don't rave to me," she said coldly, burying her curiosity. "Nothing will change the fact that you murdered a man you claimed to love."

"Yes, I killed him. I had every reason to do it. But I love him even now, God help me. Like a brother." A tear tracked from one of his blue eyes, clearing a path through the grime on his cheek.

His words just made Ellie angrier. "Robin Hood died in agony," she said, relishing the pain her words brought to Will Scarlet's face. "He was conscious till the end—he felt every minute of it. The poison killed him slowly, but he died holding his bow. Because he was a hero."

But words weren't enough. *I should just kill him*, Ellie thought. *Hurt him the way he hurt Robin.*

Then she heard Marian calling her name. The word was full of anguish, all the love Marian had shown Ellie, from the moment she gathered her to the nunnery until now, wrapped up in a shout. It jolted her back to herself.

She saw her hands, clenched and shaking around her bow, and felt the pain and exhaustion her anger had held at bay.

Ellie let her hand drop as Marian hurtled to her side, the League following behind. "I saw you kneeling," Marian said, "and I thought . . . I thought he'd . . ." Then she shook her head and straightened, shifting her gaze to Will. The rising sun was at her back, and the shape of her was tall and straight and strong.

"Tell me why you did it, Will Scarlet," Marian said. "Tell me *now*."

Still half-collapsed in the dirt, his face a mask of regret, Will Scarlet nodded.

"Five years ago," he began, "Robin stole something from the Sheriff of Nottingham."

Marian stepped forward, her eyes questioning.

"This matters, Marian," Will said quietly. "Let me tell the story how I must."

He continued, his gaze moving farther and farther away as he spoke. "It was a priceless item. A man could sell it for enough gold to live on for the rest of his days. And Robin kept it for himself."

*No.* Something deep in Ellie cried out against his words. Robin was many things—heedless, foolish at times, even arrogant. But surely he hadn't been *greedy*.

Had he?

"In order to do so," Will continued, "he had to hide it from the rest of us, from the rest of his *Merry Men*." He said the words with a bitter sneer. "He chose his hiding place recklessly—selfishly. He'd seen me hide things there a hundred times, but it was little things—a stolen trinket, a knife. And he chose that hiding spot—in the wall of my cottage."

Marian drew in a sharp breath, as if she knew where this story was going. For a moment Ellie wanted Will to stop, unsure she could bear what he would say next.

"He hid it in the wall beside our hearth, in the room where my wife and our child slept." Will's eyes narrowed. "What he didn't know was that the sheriff had him followed. He led the man right to my doorstep, Marian."

His voice had slipped into a whisper. "The sheriff had the cottage searched, and he found Robin's treasure. For the crime of its theft my wife and son were hanged on the spot. I came home too late; I could do nothing to protect them. The sheriff mocked me when I arrived—he knew the theft was Robin's doing, but he let my family pay the price. Their blood was on Robin's hands. They died, Marian, because of Robin's greed, and his thoughtlessness."

Will took a deep breath, as if he was about to say more, but fell silent.

Ellie's heart felt like a stone in her chest, heavy with pity and grief. He spoke of the man she'd thought a hero. The realization filled her with shame.

"Will," Marian said, her voice trembling. "Robin made a terrible mistake. But you misunderstood his intentions."

Ellie gasped—how could she be defending Robin even now? Will, too, tensed as he looked up at her.

Marian lifted a shaking hand and slipped it into her cloak. Then she pulled out her jeweled Bible. Will's face seemed to fold in on itself at the sight of it.

"That's it," he said hoarsely. "But how . . . how did you get . . ."

Marian's head sagged forward, as if under a great weight. "It was my Bible, Will. My mother gave it to me when I was a child, just before she died. It was the only thing of value I took from my father's house, and it fell into the sheriff's hands very early in my career as an outlaw."

She twisted her hands together, tears slipping between her lashes. "He didn't steal it out of greed, but out of love. For me. One morning, long after I'd left for the abbey, I found it waiting for me in the confessional. A robin's feather was tucked into its pages. I learned in a letter from Tuck that Robin had stolen it back again from the sheriff, at great risk. But I never knew . . . I never knew when, or what came of it."

Will's face was blank with shock; Marian leaned forward and cupped it with her hands. "Robin was always a fool, but he was never a monster. He never intended to keep that Bible for himself."

Will crumpled into himself. His body shook from the sobbing.

Tears filled Marian's eyes too. "I knew he parted from me because he was ashamed of something he'd done, and thought I'd be ashamed of him too." Her face twisted, as if her heart was breaking all over again. "Now I know what it was."

She wiped her eyes with her cloak and knelt before Will.

"I beg you," she said, "to forgive him. Forgive him for what he did, and bury your dead. And forgive yourself, for the revenge you took on him."

Will Scarlet turned his gaze, full of remorse, on Ellie. "I've had my revenge, for all the good it's done me." His voice was shocked and shaky. "Now will you take yours?"

A shudder ran through Ellie. Marian got to her feet. Neither she nor the League said a word or stepped forward to interfere. The murderer of Robin Hood, the man who'd destroyed her life, was at Ellie's mercy—but she knew revenge would do her no good. Will Scarlet's life was ruined too, by Robin's foolish decision and the sheriff's brutality. No punishment could be worse than the one he'd already lived through.

Will stared fixedly at her hand on the arrow, and she realized with a start that he *wanted* to die. It might be a mercy, then, to kill this broken man. But did she really want to take another life, not in the heat of the moment but in cold blood? Even after all he had done?

Slowly she brought her arm back . . . and tucked the silver arrow into its quiver. Will exhaled, going limp at her feet.

"Go," she said. "I forgive you. May God, too, have mercy on you."

The last she saw of Will Scarlet was his back, disappearing into a thicket of trees.

# 25

FOOTSORE AND HEARTBROKEN, THE GROUP
made their way through the forest, back toward the
village's edge.

Marian barely spoke, seeming half-lost in memories.
After fighting the baron's men and running through the
forest like a woman half her age, she now looked much
older, bowed with grief over what had been lost for the
sake of her Bible. They left her to rest in a comfortable
clearing, by a berry bush and a clear stream, promising
to return for her that night.

After Will Scarlet's confession Ellie just felt numb.
And when that wore off, the guilt crashed in once
more—she was no longer the only outlaw in the League.

For the crime of trying to help her, all of them were fugitives.

"It was our choice, Ellie," Margery said for the hundredth time. "And nobody's fault but the baron's."

"We always wanted to be outlaws," Ralf added, "just like Robin Hood. And now we've done it."

She couldn't meet his shaky smile. Margery put an arm around her, but Jacob walked with his eyes to the earth. Life as an outlaw would be hardest on him, Ellie thought. He was the only one of them who'd never had to skip a meal.

"But how will the kids get on without us?" Alice asked Ralf, the desperation in her voice like a rasp against Ellie's heart. "You know Father can't raise them alone."

"Matilda's getting older now," Ralf replied. His voice was half reassurance, half doubt. "She'll help him as much as she can. Alice, they'll be okay."

"We'll help them too," Ellie said suddenly. She stopped short on the forest path, waiting for her friends to turn and look at her. "We'll keep supporting your families no matter what. The abbey, too." She thought of Gregory Carpenter and the rest of the patients in the abbey hospital. Would they get what they needed with Mother Mary Ursula in charge? *They will if I have anything to do with it.* "I'll get food in through Sister Bethan, I know she'll risk it. We'll keep doing what we've always done: poach from the baron's lands and give the meat to those that need it."

"The new Merry Men," Alice whispered.

Some of the life came back to Jacob's eyes. "You think we could do it?" he asked hoarsely.

"We already have," Ellie said firmly. "We've stolen from the rich; we've given to the poor. We've broken into the baron's castle right under his pointy nose!"

"We've tricked his men into lying down in the dirt," Ralf added.

Alice shifted beside him. "And sneaked into a tavern," she said. "With one of us wearing the worst disguise Nottingham has ever seen."

Ellie elbowed her, but she was grinning.

"We were wrong about Will Scarlet," Jacob said. "He's not fit to be the next Robin Hood." He grinned too. "So that just leaves us."

"I'm no Robin Hood," Ellie said, squaring her shoulders. "I'm Elinor Dray. Even if I can't be the way Robin was in stories—even if nobody can—I swear I'm going to do as much good as he did. And try my best to hurt fewer people while I do it."

Ellie lingered too long in the abbey kitchen, but it was hard to go. The evening was cool, and the firelight felt good on her back. Sister Bethan's face when she saw the haunch of venison Ellie had brought her was just as warming.

Sister Bethan had laughed through the story of Ellie dressed as an old woman in no better disguise than a horse blanket, and gasped when she told her about the Greenwood Tree and the League's narrow escape from the baron's courtyard. Then she cried a little when Ellie told her about Will Scarlet's loss, and squeezed Ellie's hands.

"You gave him mercy," she said. "I couldn't be more proud of you for it. Or for this," she added, gesturing at the meat.

"How is it with Sister Mary Ursula in charge?" Ellie asked. "Is there anything else you need?"

"It's difficult without Marian," Sister Bethan said simply. "And more difficult still to see her shoes filled by such a foolish woman. But we'll make do." Her eyes flashed with something harder than mischief. "And don't you worry—things always change, Elinor, and quicker than you'd think. You know that better than anyone. Perhaps Mary Ursula won't be our mother abbess for much longer."

Ellie finally rose to leave, wondering as she did what Sister Bethan had planned for her undeserving mother abbess. Movement in the dusky yard caught her attention.

It was Gregory Carpenter, the little boy she'd last seen lying ill in the hospital. He was still sapling skinny, but even from the kitchen she could see his cheeks were rounder and warm with good health.

"Our patient has recovered his strength, I think," Sister Bethan said. They watched the boy swish a branch through the air, locked in combat with a foe they couldn't see.

"He's playing at Robin Hood and his Merry Men, isn't he?" Ellie said, grinning.

Sister Bethan looked at her. "For now, maybe. But soon I think he'll be playing at League of Archers."

Later that night Ellie lingered in the shadows of a house as her friends met their parents in the village square to say their good-byes. She could see Master Attwood's slumped shoulders, his hand patting Alice as she hugged him around the waist. Somewhere, she knew, Margery was kissing every one of her nieces and nephews good-bye, and probably the horses, too. Jacob would come back from his parents' with armfuls of arrows, at least—his father wouldn't let them go into outlawry unarmed.

"Girl. Elinor Dray."

Ellie turned quickly, her hand going to her bow.

A tall man with a gray beard approached her as you

might a skittish horse. She recognized him from the night before, from among the forces that had stormed the castle, and let her hand slip from her bow.

"I don't mean you no harm," he said. "You fought bravely last night, and I believe you had nothing to do with the death of Robin Hood."

He held out a hand, and gingerly she reached back to shake it. A woman joined him, settling under his arm.

"Thank you for all that you've done, Elinor Dray," she said softly.

More people were gathering around her now, their faces soft with gratitude—and, in some cases, touched with shame. Among them, she realized, were some of the same people who had stormed the Galpins' house or tried to seize her in the woods.

"We thank you for the coin," one woman burst out, dabbing at her eyes. "It might be enough to save us, the next time the baron comes collecting."

"The coin," Ellie repeated.

"The Attwood girl came to our houses with money—compliments of Elinor Dray and the League of Archers, she said." The bearded man's wife spoke, her voice full of wonder. "Even after we near killed you at the fletcher's house, you provided for us. It's a good thing you did, and the village won't forget."

*Does Tom Turner count as part of the village?* was Ellie's first thought. But her second was a warm relief at the thought of Alice handing out coin in the League's name. Beneath her cynic's exterior, Ellie was sure, she had the heart of an outlaw. She, like Ellie, would now be walking the path of the wolf.

When her friends' good-byes were done, they reunited with Marian deeper in the woods. Together they took the winding journey to the Greenwood Tree. This time they went slowly, treading carefully to avoid the traps that Ellie had learned to look for. Marian kept pausing to run her hand over certain trees, or break a fragrant branch or sprig of herbs from plants along the path. She smiled to herself as they walked, and Ellie pretended not to see when she patted the backs of her hands against her eyes.

It was near dawn when they arrived, the massive tree rising against a pink-veined sky. Tuck stood in the clearing beneath it. When he saw Marian, he stepped forward and folded her into his bearlike embrace. "I'm sorry about Will," he said gruffly. Marian just nodded and buried her face in his shirt.

Later, when they were eating fresh-caught fish around Tuck's campfire, Ellie finally dared ask the question that had been on her mind all day.

"We can't go back to our old lives," she said, "so

we're making new ones. We call ourselves the League of Archers, and we want to do what you did, with Robin and the Merry Men. Will you join us? And . . . and let us stay here, at the Greenwood Tree?"

Tuck took his time thinking about it, wiping his mouth and settling back onto his log with a sigh. "I don't know that the fighting life is mine to live anymore."

"Nor mine," Marian said. She looked around at the clearing, her eyes full. "There are too many memories here, of who I once was. I don't think there's room for me as I am now."

She smiled gently at Ellie's look of distress. "But this place is the perfect hideout for a band of outlaws. Tuck, what do you think?"

"I think it's the perfect home for the League of Archers, the newest threat to tyranny in Sherwood Forest. It's near impossible to find, unless you've got a tracker as keen as this one"—he pointed at Alice, who struggled not to grin—"and it'll be even safer once you've reset the traps. I'll show you how to do it."

"But where will you go?" Ellie asked.

Marian and Tuck exchanged a look. "A man of the cloth and an old abbess in disguise," Marian said lightly. "It's not the stuff of ballads, but I think we can still find some adventure." Her face grew more serious. "We'll help in any way we can. There are still so many who need care—you'll be working to feed their bodies, while the friar and I will do what we can to feed their souls."

"I've been too long in one place," the friar agreed. "We'll be of more use if we take to the road."

The ghosts that haunted Marian's greenwood must have been loud ones—she and Tuck set out before the sun was at its height. Before climbing into Tuck's cart, she stood before Ellie and cupped her face in her palms.

"You've already done so much good, Elinor Dray," she murmured. "I look forward to hearing about all the good you've yet to do."

Ellie was struck with a sudden desire to cling to Marian. With the abbess gone, Ellie would be alone in the woods.

But she wasn't alone. She looked around—Jacob stood by the cart, resting his weight on a staff. Margery was at the horse's head, feeding it a carrot. And Ralf and Alice were making ready to follow Tuck on foot, so he could show them how to work the traps.

She took a deep breath and hugged Maid Marian, trying to soak up all the courage she could from her embrace. "Thank you for taking me in," she whispered. "Thank you for being my home."

"I won't go far," the abbess whispered back. "If you need me, you'll find a way to let me know."

Then she pulled away and climbed onto Tuck's cart, just another traveler in the costume of an old maid.

Three days later Ellie knelt in the shrubbery by the side of the Nottingham road. The sun was low, and she thought it might be time for the compline prayer. As she uttered the prayer's familiar words, Ellie tried not to imagine Mother Mary Ursula leading the nuns in prayer. She ended with a prayer of her own: for the safety of her friends, and for the skill and grace to complete the task at hand.

Then she stood and stretched, looking back at the rest of the League where they stood patiently waiting.

"You ready?"

They nodded, just as the approaching rumble of a cart sent them into the bushes and trees clustered along the bend in the road.

Ellie peered down from a crook in a small apple tree and smiled. It was the cart they'd been waiting for. When it came close enough, she could hear the accented chatter of the people who rode in it, and see the purple of their cloaks.

"Now!" she said, jumping down onto the path. Five arrows flew into the cart, and the Frenchmen's conversation turned to panicked shouts. The cart veered wildly as the driver ducked from a second hail of arrows, then stopped hard against the trunk of a juniper.

Not a drop of blood spilled, Ellie noted with satisfaction. Ten arrows pinned four Frenchmen down by their cloaks. Alice and Ellie kept arrows aimed on the silent men as Jacob, Margery, and Ralf quickly unloaded heavy sacks and boxes from the cart bed.

"I thank you for your cooperation," Ellie said cheerfully, sighting down her arrow at the men's enraged faces, some of them nearly as purple as their cloaks. "But it seems there's been a mistake. The money you carry is destined for *your* king, King Philip."

She paused on a man whose fingers were creeping for the knife at his belt, and watched him stony eyed till he reluctantly lifted his hand.

"You see," she continued, "the baron has already used Kirklees's money to buy his soldiers—in the name of King John. No one man can side with two kings, not even a baron. So we're taking *this* money and returning it to its rightful owners."

One of the men finally slipped free of his cloak and slowly stood, his hands by his ears. "We know nothing of your local politics," he spat. "We only know what the baron told us. This was his betrayal, not ours."

Ellie shrugged and moved closer as Ralf began tying

the man's hands behind his back. "It appears you, too, are a victim of the baron's treachery. I suggest you think of that before you side with him again."

As the final man's hands were tied, she unhitched the horses from the cart and sent them on their way with a hard slap to the rump.

"We're the League of Archers," she cried. "And you can send Lord de Lays our compliments."

Then she bowed and ran into the woods, her friends by her side.

# ABOUT THE AUTHOR

When she's not writing, Eva Howard escapes the city to hike and camp in the forest—and has even tried her hand at archery. She lives in New York.